BLAZING LIGHT

TALES FROM THE EDGE - BOOK 3

CHLOE ADLER

Signum
Publishing

COPYRIGHT

BLAZING LIGHT BY CHLOE ADLER

Book 3 - Tales From the Edge

Want a FREE Novella? Subscribe to Chloe's newsletter!

Fire and Fangs is a sexy, enemies to lovers, multiple partner paranormal with sword-crossing. Subscribe to my newsletter to grab it!
https://BookHip.com/QFGLCWZ

ISBN: 978-1-947156-16-6

© Cover Art: 2024 Rebeca Covers
Editor: Elizabeth Nover - Razor Sharp Editing

CHAPTER ONE

THORN

As the demon and I fall through the portal, I have time to ponder how this space could be utterly devoid of light. Even my keen eyesight picks up nothing, not a pinprick, not a shade of gray.

One minute I was on the beach, following my cousin Nolan. My biggest decision as a small dragon the size of a housecat was which tasty insect to stalk and munch on. But then the sea parted, and this red-eyed, horned beast from another world tried to intimidate Nolan into giving up our girl. He didn't. I'm proud of his refusal, though I would have clawed out his eyes if he'd given the demon any other answer. When the demon reached for him, I acted on instinct and apparently so did it, pulling me into its world.

After moments in free fall, I pull my claws free of its

hold and I spread my wings to break my fall, still sailing downward but as far from the demon as I can get. Flying around in a vacuum is less than ideal. And the smell! My snout picks up only char and decay. I breathe out fire to light my way, but it illuminates nothing beyond the outline of my wings in the darkness.

After what is probably only moments but feels like an eternity, my feet hit the ground. Except it breaks apart under my talons like dried leaves. I bend down to inhale and wish I hadn't. Immediately I sneeze and cough, trying to drive the thick and foul stench from my throat.

"What's that?" comes a tiny little voice to one side.

"A beast from another dimension," says another, a little more nasal than the first.

They sound like damned Smurfs. I can't distinguish their gender, not that it matters. Unfortunately, I can't speak and I still can't see, so I stay put. If they try and hurt me, I can take flight, but if I step left or right, I might stomp one of them.

"Maybe it's come to save us."

I nod my head on the off chance they can see me.

"Did you see that?"

"Was that a nod?"

I nod again.

Sounds of crunching and crackling fill the air, which is as dense as Jell-O.

A tiny little hand touches the side of my neck. "One nod for yes and two for no," says the owner of the hand.

I wait.

"This is where you test it, dunce," says the other with a sigh. "Here, let me do it."

Another tiny hand touches the other side of my neck. I make sure to hold very still.

"Nod twice for no," says the voice.

I do.

"Now once for yes."

I nod once.

"It understands."

"Obviously."

"My name is Astra," says the first voice.

"And I'm Basil," says the nasal one.

Great. I can't talk, so I merely nod.

"You came through a portal from the world beyond?" asks Astra.

I nod, tiring of this game.

"Well," says Basil, "wherever you came from is far better than here."

"Yeah," says Astra on a sigh, "welcome to hell."

I stiffen. What the?

3

"Goodness, don't scare the guy." He leans close to my ear. "It's not really hell."

She grunts. "It is now, thanks to the Scrim."

"Shhh. You trying to get yourself killed?"

"The dragon will protect me." She pets the side of my neck. "Won't you, boy?"

I find myself nodding. Any enemy of what I suspect is the demon who sent me here is a friend of mine. And though I can't see these creatures, their hands are so tiny and their voices so high-pitched they must be about the size of the demon's middle finger.

"Yup, yup, compared to you, we're small," she says as though she can read my thoughts. "But the Scrim used to be our size too." Her tiny hand smooths down my scales.

The motion is soothing, hypnotic, and despite myself, I start to relax. I like these creatures. They're nice. She's petting me in just the right spot! My leg twitches and paws the air. Astra pulls her hand away and I almost fall over, sucking in a deep breath to steady myself. I cough, practically shooting out a jet of fire.

"Careful," says Basil.

"It's not like he can scorch the ground anymore. But don't breathe too deeply," she says to me. "That monster destroyed our world. There's nothing left but ash and it sticks in your lungs."

"Causes ash-lung," Basil adds.

"And you don't want that." She pats the side of my neck.

Not if it feels anything close to what I'm already experiencing now, I don't.

"You can say that again," she says.

Say what?

"You'll help us right everything, won't you?" Astra purrs, stroking my neck again.

Of course I will! *Yes, yes, yes!* I want to yell but I nod furiously instead.

"Our savior." She plants a tiny kiss on my scales and I beam.

About time someone saw me as that. But wasn't I doing something in my own world? Don't I have family there? But that's silly, Astra and Basil are my family. No matter. I'm here with these two adorable . . . whatever they're called now and this is where I shall stay.

"We're pixies," she says. "How rude of me not to ask for your name."

Thorn.

Basil touches the other side of my neck. "Thorn, what a perfect name for you."

You *can* hear my thoughts?

"Of course we can," she giggles, the sound like wind chimes in a soft ocean breeze.

"Here, we'll lead you to our house," says Basil.

Oh, yes please.

"He can't fit in our house, Basil."

"Oh," he giggles. "Right, he's too big. He'll sleep outside and guard us."

Of course I will.

"And in the morning, we'll teach him how to defeat the Scrim and bring back our light."

I'd do anything for you two.

Iphigenia

*R*hys drives me to the circus for my performance. We hold hands but neither of us speaks, as if he senses I need the time to center myself. I run through my routine in my head and try to push away the week's drama, but it seeps right back in—the good, the bad and the delicious. I'm now a woman with three serious boyfriends. Nope, still sounds crazy. How do I even introduce everyone? I let out a small sigh. The important, wonderful thing is that all my men are happy with our arrangement, though I do wonder if everything will remain copacetic moving forward. I did just add Dominic to our mix, after all.

As though he can read my mind, Rhys squeezes my hand. Little does he know that *I'm* the mind reader, but I trust Dominic not to spill that secret.

I peer out the window, watching the trees give way to the ocean as we turn onto Discovery Highway. The moon is bright, lighting the water with a brilliance that can only be described as nature's magic.

"Are you worried about your show or are you thinking about the demon?" Rhys tightens his grip on my hand.

Neither. "Hopefully the demon is contained, for now."

"At least you've found a way to help those ghouls become human again. And the Signum." His dark hair falls across his forehead, making him appear even more kissable. I lean over and peck his cheek when he turns back to the road. A broad smile creases his face.

He's right, I should focus more on the positive and less on the drama. I was able to help some of those ghouls. Maybe I *can* stop the trauma in our town.

"Have you heard from your brother?" I focus on his dark eyes but they don't veer toward me or give any indication of how he's feeling.

He shakes his head. "No, Nolan hasn't called me. At least Thorn is with him. I'm sure after a while, he'll be fine. He used to go off like this when we were kids too."

It must be difficult having a brother like that. Since they were recently reunited, Rhys has worked so hard to make Nolan feel like part of the family again, but he seems determined to remain alienated.

Rhys turns into the boardwalk parking lot and stops the car. Leaning toward me, he pats his chest and I lunge into his embrace. His muscular arms wrap around me and hold me close, stroking the back of my head. I jerk away. "No mussing the curls."

"How 'bout a kiss?" His eyes crinkle at the corners and I drop my lips on his.

His mouth is wet and hot, the kiss intense. He gives me his full attention, leaning me back against the seat of the car and probing my mouth deeper. My answering kiss is ferocious. I need to cement my solo connection with Rhys. Last night when we made love, it was a foursome and all my men were amazing. Rhys, Dominic and Caspian played perfectly together with me as their focus. But now I crave time alone with each one. After everything we've been through over the past few weeks, I need to reconnect.

He stops kissing me to hold my gaze and I clamber on top of him, straddling his legs and heaving myself against his rock-hard cock, grinding my wet core into his.

I rock back, and his eyelids fall to half-mast.

"Let me." My breath is tight, I'm practically panting.

"Whatever you want, I'm here. I'm yours," he growls and tries to pull my mouth back to his, but I hold back.

"Hold still." I buck into him, a slow, punishing rhythm. With every push of my hips his cock expands until it's pulsing against his jeans. I use his bulge, grinding down hard against it, and the scorching heat radiates up from my pussy and out through my extremities. I claw at his shoulders, riding his captive cock with my covered pussy.

"The smell of you is driving me wild," he growls.

Instead of responding, I increase my pace, desperate to come with him here in this parking lot, claiming him as mine even through our clothes.

As my orgasm crests I latch my mouth onto his, riding him through my convulsions and his.

I groan, the sound guttural in my ears, while my fingers grate down his chest and my orgasm rockets through me. A long moment later, I ease up, pushing softly against his now-spent dick, and then collapse on him. I nuzzle into his neck, burying my face there.

"How long has it been since you've fed?" I ask without pulling back to look at him.

"Since you."

"How much longer can you go?"

He wets his lips. "I can taste the sweet syrup of your breath."

"That's not an answer."

"A few more days."

"Drink from me?"

He cups my face in his hands and forces me to look at him. "There's a reason vampires have four donors a month."

I bite my lip. "I know. Are you interviewing any new donors?"

He brushes his thumb over my lip, releasing it. "I should, but I wanted to wait and talk to you about it. I know the last time I brought it up you weren't entirely comfortable and I want you to be. I *need* you to be."

I smile and kiss him softly. "I spoke to Chrys about it at length. She was able to put it in perspective. It's who you are and I accept all parts of you. I trust you. So please, do whatever you need to do." I reach out and brush a sweaty lock of hair off his forehead.

He pulls my face back to his and licks the crease of my lips, his tongue flicking between them before planting a hard kiss. I push back into him, biting at his lips and sucking them in, warmth and light filling me up. We make out for a few seconds longer before I hop off and pull down the visor to fix my hair.

He gets out of the car and goes around the other side to open mine. Such a gentleman. He extends his hand, and I take it. He walks me through the lot and down the pier to the big top tent.

"We'll all be watching you." He bends to kiss me again and our mouths come together like a lock and key.

"I love you," I whisper.

"I love you too, Iphigenia, the light of my life. Of all our lives." He squeezes me and lets go.

I walk into the tent without looking back because I know he's standing there, watching me, and if I see the way he's no doubt looking at me, I'll throw tonight's performance to the wind and run to him instead.

CHAPTER TWO

CASPIAN

*R*hys is waiting on the pier for us and we all go to Confections to pick out a treat for her after her performance. Then we peruse the shops to kill time before the show starts. We haven't lived here long enough to get bored of the pier shops yet, and my camera is always at the ready to catch the glint of the sun off the water, waves playing against the sunlight and sailboats tripping along the surf as they pull into the harbor.

"How was Iphigenia feeling before you dropped her off?" asks Dom.

Rhys winks at both of us. "Pretty damn good."

"Dog." I clip his shoulder.

"At least she'll be relaxed." Dom grins.

We make our way inside the big top and take seats a few rows back from the front. We don't want to distract our girl but we also know it's important for her to know we're here.

The lights dim and the audience hushes. I move forward, excitement sparking through my veins. I've been allowed by the owner, Serlon, to photograph this particular performance and I check to make sure I have the correct lens and settings, a constant adjustment.

The curtains part to reveal Alexis, the master of ceremonies. I train the lens on her, checking that the aperture and focus are correct in the dim light. Although the circus boasts two themes per season, there are often little differences between each performance to keep the crowds coming back, night after night, weekend after weekend. And Serlon promised this performance would be particularly photogenic.

Dressed in a demure schoolgirl outfit, Alexis stands with her arms raised above her head. When she drops them down in one grand flourish, the house lights click off and darkness descends over the auditorium. We gasp, collectively caught off guard, as Alexis's outfit flares to life with patterns and shapes that glow in the dark. Even her makeup lights up her cheeks in freckles.

As she walks in a slow circle around the stage, the sound of chains unraveling fills the space. One thick aluminum-chain rope drops from the ceiling above us, also lit with the glow-in-the-dark paint.

Center stage now, Alexis clutches a link in a chain with one hand and rises as its course is reversed. She wraps the thick links around her middle, then mimes swimming through the air, just a carefree girl out for a swim in the peaceful ocean. But after a moment, her movements turn frantic, as if struggling against a rip tide, and then her whole body goes limp, hanging still with her tongue lolling out of her mouth.

The audience gasps and another chain drops with a loud clang. The house lights blaze on again. Suspended at the top of the tent is Iphigenia, her back arched and her whole body spinning in a wide circle, the chain trailing down behind her. A white gossamer tail spreads out behind her tight, one-piece mermaid outfit. A large crown of shells interwoven with pearls perches above her perfect blond ringlets. The crowd roars, standing and cheering her name. I stand with them, moving into the aisle to snap photos now that there's more light.

Iphi performs a flawless routine that simulates being underwater. With every climb, she spreads her arms in a stroke and with every fall she holds her legs together while her body spins in tight circles.

Our eyes follow her every movement from the top of the chain to the bottom and then back up again.

All at once, Iphi catches sight of schoolgirl Alexis, her inert form still collapsed in the center of the other chain. The distraught mermaid stops her spinning and climbs down toward the other woman. When she reaches Alexis's height, Iphi leaps from her chain to the other—to the audience's audible delight. I click and capture the leap in midair. Down on my little screen, Iphi is perfectly posed even during the leap. When the hell did she find time to practice this routine?

She lands just above Alexis and removes her crown of shells, attaching it to the other girl's head. And just like that, the drowned schoolgirl straightens and sparks back to life. Iphi reaches for her hand and the woman grasps hers back. With every movement, Alexis becomes more animated, swimming through the air with renewed vigor. Iphi removes her gossamer tail and, climbing around the other woman, attaches it to Alexis's back. Then, with a tug and some stage magic, the gossamer fabric turns into iridescent scales to match Iphi's own tights. The chain falls away from the lower half of Alexis's body, her new tail wrapping around her legs in its place. The two women, now both mermaids, spin together, Alexis holding on to Iphi's forearm.

Their circle widens and Iphi swings back to her own chain while Alexis swims away, her chain pulled up into the rafters.

Iphi twirls and climbs one last time before performing a dismount that looks like a triple back flip. She sticks to the white stage floor, her arms raised high, and everyone stands to applaud. I snap a few more shots but before the applause has a chance to die down, ropes descend from the rafters just as the chains did. I freeze with my camera trained on Iphi, surprised they're going directly into the next act. Half a dozen figures, all dressed in black, descend together from the roof.

That's when Iphi screams.

Iphigenia

*a*t least I'm alone on the stage when the ghouls descend from the rafters. No time to wonder how they're so agile as they surround me. Really? I'm being attacked on stage *again*? I had finally worked through all my anxiety from the last time I was attacked during a show. First Trackers, now ghouls—are they sharing a freaking villain playbook?

Without a second to waste I leap back up onto the chain and climb, rung after rung, hauling myself skyward. After my third handhold one of the ghouls leaps for my legs and catches my feet. But—thank you, Alexis—I'm used to climbing both without the use of my legs and with dead weight attached. I'm even able to look down and survey the chaotic scene below.

My men bellow below me, rushing onto the stage while most of the audience scatters for the exits. Thanks to the Edge's municipal codes, no one is allowed to shift here, but that doesn't stop my men from riding to my rescue. Dominic shouts something at a stagehand, who nods and runs backstage. A moment later, the rigging from all the other acts yet to go tonight drop down from the rafters at once. Dominic and Caspian start yanking down ropes and silk streamers—why?—while Rhys barks into his phone.

I keep climbing, flinging my legs back and forth. The ghoul tightens its grip on my calves, but it's slipping and I don't want to be the cause of its death. If I can get it off now, it's only a fifteen-foot drop—way better than a fall from the catwalk above. So I yank my legs into a half twist and shoot my body toward the roof. The sheer force of my lunge sends him flying free, and I use the momentum to climb even higher.

Sirens flow up the pier; I've never been so happy to be so close to the station. I perch high atop the chain and watch the men fight below. Rhys, his phone long gone, is using his moves on the ghouls still coming at him. He ducks, throws out a leg and sweeps it under the closest attacker. The ghoul goes down with a thunk and Caspian is on top of it with a rope. Rhys goes for the next one, who lunges for his throat, hands out. He pivots to the side and the ghoul crashes off the stage and falls into the stands. Dominic jumps off the stage and lands on top of him, wrenching his hands over his head to secure them with a silk cuff.

By the time the police arrive, a mere two minutes later, my men have disabled and restrained all six ghouls. Still, officers surround them, guns drawn.

"Any vampires among the mix?" Chief Sheldon asks Caspian.

"Rhys?" Cas looks at his cousin, who shakes his head.

"No sir, they're all human." Guilt steams off Rhys in a cloud visible only to me. It's no surprise; he made these ghouls himself when he was under the

Scrim's control. Of course he was able to predict their moves.

Thirty minutes and one de-ghoulification spell from yours truly later, a troop of officers loads the former ghouls into the back of a police van. They'll be taken to the hospital for a medical checkup, then the station for statements. Sheldon asks to talk to us outside for a minute, and though I'm about to fall over with fatigue from so much physical and magical exertion, I can hardly tell him no.

"Why do you think they attacked in the middle of a performance?" He holds a pad of paper in one hand and a pen in the other.

Rhys growls. "Because they don't have a brain between the six of them."

Sheldon shakes his head. "They're getting bolder for a reason."

"Maybe they thought they could grab her quickly?" says Caspian. "Maybe they wanted an audience when they did so?"

"Like they were trying to make a statement." Dominic puts an arm around me. " 'We can kidnap your people from right under your nose.' "

"Perhaps they *had* to attack me here. It was one of the first places I warded, so it must be the first place for the spell to wane. If only there was a visible timestamp on magic spells." Or if only I was as powerful as my mother. I chew on my lower lip.

The Scrim was sending a message *to me*. He was showing me that I'd better come willingly or he'll ramp up his efforts to terrorize my entire town. Someone could have been hurt tonight, like Alexis, and it would have been my fault. I can't keep just reacting to the problem. I need to *solve* it. Time to end this. Time to find my own way into Brae.

Rhys puts an arm around my other shoulder and Caspian stands behind me, wending his arms around my waist.

Sheldon looks up from his notepad and makes eye contact with each of the guys. "Take care of her."

"We will," they reply in unison and then pivot to walk me back to the tent so I can change and grab my stuff.

CHAPTER THREE

CASPIAN

t home, Iphigenia lets out a heavy sigh. She drops on the couch with Rhys on her left. Dom sits on the floor by her feet, looking up at her and using his most soothing psychologist voice. It used to irk the hell out of me, but I've grown to appreciate it. Especially in moments like these, when it's calming our girl.

"We'll figure this out together." Dom's hands rest on her knees. "There's no reason to go at it by yourself."

"We want to help," I call from the kitchen, where I'm making Iphi some much-needed herbal tea.

"Please let us," Rhys says.

I hand her the warm mug and sit on her right. I had almost forgotten she was attacked during a circus performance once, long before any of us knew her. Her silks were cut by terrorists, and she tumbled many feet to the ground and broke a leg. It took her months to recover and another year before she was comfortable performing again. Then tonight happened. All of that progress destroyed like a burnt-up Polaroid. If anyone can help her get past it, Dominic can.

She clutches her tea in both hands and smiles at me, but it's perfunctory and doesn't reach those cerulean eyes. Eyes that currently remind me of sea glass caught in the tumble of an ocean tsunami. Pink suffuses her cheeks as she breathes in the steam rising from the cup, her perfect nose turned up, her blond curls falling in mismatched lengths. Post-performance hair. I want to take her face in my hands and kiss her cheeks, her eyes, her perfect little nose, and push back her fear with pleasure.

There's a knock on the door and we all startle. Dom pushes himself up but the knob turns and a wild-eyed Nolan bursts inside.

"Thorn!" he screams.

The rest of us jump to our feet.

Dominic approaches the crazed vamp, his hands held out. "What's wrong?"

"He took Thorn." Nolan's gaze swings between us, his eyes bloodshot and raw.

"Who took Thorn?" asks Dominic.

"The Scrim."

Iphigenia's mouth opens and closes like a fish out of water. The mug crashes to the floor, tea splashing everywhere. Her eyes close and squeeze shut like she's trying to shut out the world. After everything she's been through tonight, and now this too. I pick up the mug, still whole, and drop it on the coffee table. Then I put my arm around her, pulling her into me. She leans her head against me, which only exacerbates the sound of her heart thumping wildly in her chest.

Dominic holds his hands out. "One thing at a time Nolan, please." His calming timbre works on me and Iphigenia too. Her heartbeat slows a fraction, and she lets out a tiny mewl. "Where and when?"

Nolan runs his hands through his hair. "It's my fault. I couldn't stop him."

Rhys puts his arm around his brother's shoulders. "Hey man, whatever happened, there was nothing you could have done. But . . . who is the Scrim?"

It's Iphi who responds, though she doesn't pull away from my chest to do it, her voice muffled. "No one knows exactly, but he's evil. He lives in some other dimension. He tried to kidnap Sadie once, years ago. My f-father gave his life to banish him to his home world."

She stops talking for a moment, and I squeeze her closer still, trying to share my strength with her. How hard it must be for her to dredge up these memories.

"He must be the puppet master, the one making all the ghouls here on Earth to do his bidding. I guess it was too much of a coincidence for there to be two powerful bad guys attacking the Edge. But . . . *why*? Why is he back? And why now? And why hasn't he tried to go after Sadie again?"

"Let's go and ask him," I snarl. "Where did this occur? Maybe the portal is still open."

Nolan shakes his head. "It happened hours ago, I think. I must have passed out afterward. It was on the beach. The portal was over the water, and I dove into the surf to try and grab Thorn, but then . . . nothing. I just came to in the sand, dry, like the tide had gone out while I was unconscious. I got here as fast as I could."

"But . . ." Iphi looks around me at Nolan. "Are you sure?"

"I don't know any other giant, bald, shark-toothed monster that can open a portal and drag someone inside of it. Do you?" His voice is shaking.

"Hey now," Rhys squeezes his shoulder, "no need to get snarky."

"I'm sorry. I'm frustrated and pissed at myself," Nolan growls.

Iphi untangles herself from me and rushes up the ladder of the loft. "I'm changing into something more utilitarian," she calls down.

"Sit down while Iphi dresses." Dominic motions to a stool. "Let me get you some coffee."

Rhys steers his brother to a seat.

Poor Nolan. He's been through far too much in the past couple of years and he's always looked up to Thorn. God, Thorn. How can he be gone? Witnessing the Scrim take our pack leader would mess any of us up. Just hearing about it after the fact cuts me to the core. And yet, of all of us, Thorn has the best chance of coming out on top against that monster.

"Cas, fill some water bottles and throw some snacks into the backpack in case we need anything," Dominic says.

I open the hall closet and grab a daypack, filling it with supplies. Water bottles, jerky, trail mix, a coil of rope, a hefty utility knife, a first-aid kit. You never know. We'll stop off at Thorn's on the way to grab his gun belt too so we have at least one gun and a can of mace.

"What's the plan?" I ask.

"Nolan, can you bring us to the exact spot where Thorn was taken?" asks Rhys.

Nolan downs the entire cup of coffee and shakes his head miserably. "Even if we could figure out how to open it in the middle of the ocean, it's on a public beach." He looks at me.

I nod. "Could attract spectators. Someone could get hurt."

"How about trying the one in the forest?" Dom asks. "It's close and it's private."

"Yeah." Nolan rakes his hands through his disheveled dark hair the same way his brother does. "I can take you to that one."

"When's the last time you ate?" Rhys asks.

Nolan looks at him with red-rimmed eyes and shakes his head.

"I'll do it." Iphigenia bounds down the loft ladder in jeans and a hoodie. Could she look any more gorgeous? I doubt it.

"No," we all say in unison.

"My blood, my choice." She walks over to Nolan and sits on the empty stool next to him.

Rhys leans across and shakes his head at her. "You need more time to replenish. I drank from you less than a week ago."

She narrows her eyes at him. "I eat plenty of beets and black beans. I'll just add some iron supplements this week too." Holding her wrist out to Nolan, she smiles. "Please, sweetheart, take what you need."

Nolan looks between her eyes and her wrist. I growl and lurch forward but Dominic holds out an arm, barring my way. "Let her."

What the hell? I lean close to his ear. "We're supposed to protect her."

He turns his head toward mine. "We're supposed to let her make her own decisions and stand by in case she gets hurt."

I growl. Damn psychologist.

"Fine." I cross my arms over my chest and glare between Nolan and Dom. They both ignore me. Nolan is still eyeing her wrist as though it's a steak. Well, more like a veggie burger, since he is a vegetarian when he bothers to eat food. If there were other known hybrids in the world besides Nolan and Rhys, perhaps we'd know more about how much blood their vampire half truly needs to sustain them versus how much food powers their shifts. But all we have to go on is physical appearance and crankiness. And Nolan is definitely cranky.

"It's okay." Iphigenia pushes her wrist toward his lips and our cousin latches on without another pause. He drinks slowly, deliberately, looking up into her eyes every minute and waiting until she nods before continuing. After a few minutes he stops. Rhys hands him a black napkin and he wipes his lips.

"Thank you." Color steeps his face. His eyes are clear and no longer red. "I didn't realize how much I needed food . . ." He looks at Rhys who shakes his head once. "Blood. I didn't realize how much I needed blood."

"It's okay." Iphigenia touches his shoulder. "I understand."

The look he gives her makes me want to leap across the small space and punch him in his face. Ours!

"Can you take us to the portal now?" asks Rhys, and Nolan nods. He rises, rubs his hands on his jeans and looks at each one of us in turn. Dom slings the backpack over his shoulder, and we all follow Nolan outside, stopping at Thorn's for his gun belt.

On the way to the tree that opened into a portal not that long ago, Nolan tells us what happened to Thorn. "The demon—the Scrim—was floating outside the portal. He had me by my wrists and was trying to pull me back inside, but Thorn . . ." He stops walking and blinks, looking away from us. "He saved my life. But in doing so, the demon pulled him back into his world, into Brae. And they disappeared together."

Iphigenia strides forward to catch up to him. "What is Brae? Is that the name of his home world?"

"Yes. It's not just another world, though. It's another realm, outside of this one."

"You've been there?" I move to the other side of him.

"I have but only for a short time, when he made . . ." Something desolate moves below his features. "When he made me an anchor. It was blacker than the darkest night."

Iphigenia loops an arm through his and Dominic puts his hand on my shoulder to stop my reaction. I force myself to relax.

"Did you see anyone else when you were there?" Her voice is breathless.

"No, it was too dark. I couldn't see anything at all."

"We know the puppet master—the Scrim—can't come here on his own now. But why? He's done it before." She swallows hard, then juts her chin forward. Trying to power through a bad memory?

I exchange looks with Dominic. Iphi's father gave his life to send the demon back to its world forever. Instead, he only bought his daughters a short reprieve? That's brutal.

Nolan licks his lips, full and red with her blood. "He needs Signum anchors to subvert whatever it is that bars him from this world, but it costs him energy. I was one of those anchors, but he can only spend a few minutes here per anchor. That's why he keeps trying to make more, why he took Rhys."

"And he uses the Signum anchors to control the ghouls," adds Rhys.

A true puppet master indeed.

"But why here? Why not somewhere else?" Iphigenia asks and Nolan shakes his head, stopping at a tree.

"I think it may have something to do with your mother," Rhys says.

Iphigenia

"*M*y mother? That doesn't even make sense. Why would you say that?" I unhook my arm from Nolan's. The others stop and wait.

"He mumbled something about a witch and her evil eyes," Rhys says, shaking his head. "I'm sorry, I spaced on it until just now. Maybe he was confused and talking about someone else."

"Or maybe you're right about Aurelia and that's why he wants you," Caspian says.

Mom's eyes are distinctive. Not evil, but memorable. Though it would make more sense if he was talking about Sadie, the witch he went after last time. But as lovely as Sadie is, her eyes are hardly her most distinguishing feature. No, he'd rant about her bright red hair. Is it really possible? Could this have something to do with our mother? But if it's true, that answer only leads to more questions.

"Great. He's completely delusional, not just someone with delusions of grandeur." Dominic drops the backpack and then unclips a can of riot-control mace from Thorn's gun belt. He also unclips the gun holster before handing me the mace.

"What now?" I take the canister from him and hold it in my hand just to be agreeable. It's cold and small and I hate the feel of it in my hand. I have my own pepper spray—a gift from Aurelia—but I don't like to carry it and thankfully have never had to use it. Though I did come close once when Nolan was a rogue anchor.

"Can we just summon the demon?" Caspian shrugs, his arms out and palms up.

I shake my head. "We need the element of surprise so we can sneak in and get Thorn without the Scrim knowing. Yes?"

"I can open the portal." Nolan raises his chin and moves in front of the tree. Resting his palms on it, he closes his eyes.

Dominic removes the gun from Thorn's holster, steps to the side and trains it on the tree trunk. We wait for several minutes.

Nothing happens.

"Open the portal," Nolan says. "Door open." He rubs his hands against the bark. Nothing happens. "Shit. I used to be able to open this."

"But you're no longer an anchor," says Rhys.

No, but *I* am a witch. My family is world renowned for its powerful, elaborate spells. Surely if my mother and sisters can change people's forms, I can open a portal that Nolan, who is no witch, was able to open. I may not be an anchor for the Scrim, but he does seem to want me and maybe that's enough.

I hand the mace to Rhys, then rest a hand on Nolan's shoulder. "Here, let me try."

"Wait." Dominic hands his weapon to Caspian and rummages in the backpack, pulling out the rope. "May I?"

He holds it up to me and I nod.

He wraps the rope around my waist several times, then knots it tightly. "Why did you give the mace to Rhys?" He holds his hand out to Rhys but I shake my head.

"I'd rather not have a weapon. That may just piss him off more." Though the plain truth is that I just don't want to use it. Being an empath makes it nearly impossible to inflict pain on others as I physically experience it myself. But even if that weren't true, I'm nonviolent down to my core. I may not qualify as a complete pacifist—I'd fight for my friends and family, even a stranger if I had to—but it's always a last resort.

I tug on the rope around my belly. "I'm ready."

Dominic grabs the other end of it and I switch places with Nolan, putting my own hands on the tree trunk. I wish I had a new amulet, but for now, I pray the protection spell my mother put over me still holds.

"*Aperta portal, aperta portal, aperta portal.*"

Nothing happens.

I turn to look at the others. Hmm. More juice? No time to set up a magic circle, but . . . "Can you all recite the chant with me?"

"Of course," says Rhys.

"*Aperta portal.*" And the men repeat after me until we are all chanting together.

Nothing. Absolutely nothing.

"It's not working." I place my hands on my hips and pout. The men stop chanting.

"Now what?" asks Dominic.

"I don't know. We stop and regroup I guess." My chin slumps against my chest and I squeeze my eyes shut. I'm not equipped for this but I'm not about to give up either. I'll do whatever it takes. Talk to my mother, to my sisters. There's got to be a way in.

"Something's happening," Caspian says and I look up as the bark shifts and ripples, forming a tiny whirlpool in the center that grows larger before our eyes.

When the door opens, I freeze. I'm not the one who opened it. I leap away as the face of the monster appears, all teeth and glittering black eyes.

"You rang?" He laughs and reaches out a clawed hand, wrapping it around my wrist and pulling me inside. So much for my mother's protection spell and the element of surprise.

The rope pulls taut over my ribcage. "Slack!" I manage to yell as I'm sucked through the portal and into the darkness beyond.

CHAPTER FOUR

DOMINIC

The weight of Iphi falling drags me along the forest floor, but before I am sucked inside too, the portal slams shut and my face meets the bark. Wham. Ouch.

The rest of the men yell, drop their weapons and grab the rope, yanking it back but it doesn't budge. I peel myself off the tree and hold up a hand, fist closed. They stop pulling.

"Let out some more slack," I order and we inch the rope forward in our hands. Even though the tree trunk looks to be solid wood once more, the rope feeds easily into it.

"Shouldn't we pull her out?" Rhys asks.

"I don't think we can. She's going to have to open it again from her side and we don't want to slam her up against the other side of the barrier." I rub my forehead.

"But we can't open it," says Caspian.

"We're screwed," says Rhys.

"Hey guys, calm down. Iphi's resourceful. As long as this rope holds taut, we know she's on the other side doing her thing." I try to keep my voice even, though I feel like screaming and beating my hands against the tree trunk or finding some dynamite to blow it up with. I force my jaw to relax so I'm not talking through clenched teeth. "Plus, Thorn's in there and he won't let anything happen to her."

Caspian nods, and Rhys takes a deep breath before nodding as well. It's like Thorn's name is a talisman even in his absence, banishing fear and calming us all. There isn't a more protective soul in the universe when it comes to family. Even when he was a kid, Thorn would do everything he could to keep us safe.

So we'll just take a breath and let Iphi do her thing, because somewhere on the other side, Thorn has her back.

Once, I was up in a hot air balloon with him and Dad. It was a rare family outing, before Cas was born. I was too young to know Dad had other lives, other women, other families.

Thorn and I were so excited. He must have

traded that balloon ride for something; they are not cheap. In retrospect, I'm sure he gave the guy something illegal. Or did something illegal for it. Doesn't matter now, it's not like I can ask him.

We took off in a blur of heat and noise. In between the bursts of fire, what I remember the most is the silence. The awe of it all. We leaned far over the basket's edge, surveying the world below. Dad was in an unusual mood. Not foul. Mom, who was afraid of heights, giggled and jumped up and down like a schoolgirl, her arm loose around his waist.

"I could power this thing." Thorn eyed the burner and the pilot scoffed. Thorn had recently learned to shift but only into his small dragon shift, and only once.

"I'd like to see that," said the pilot. A wiry man with cropped white hair.

"So would I," Dad snarled, pulling away from Mom and crowding Thorn. The mood in the basket soured. Mom gasped and shrank into me.

"I was just k-kidding." Thorn was only a boy. We both were. But Dad's anger had no boundaries. No sides. All sharp corners.

"Always trying to show me up." Dad leaned down, putting his face close to Thorn's, who backed away, caught at the edge of the basket.

"Nicolas, no," Mom screamed but no one was prepared for what happened next. He pivoted on his heel toward me, grabbed me by the collar, and in an instant I was airborne over the side.

I was too shocked to even scream, too scared to breathe. Even as my body went weightless, my heart turned to stone, as if it suddenly weighted a ton and was yanking me straight to the desert terrain below.

Mom scrambled to the edge and shoved Dad aside, but it was too late. He was a brute to us kids but never to her. She could stand up to him. Even her fear of looking down didn't stop her. Thorn told me later she leaped up onto the railing, and the pilot had to run over and haul her down.

It was just the distraction Thorn needed. As I flailed and fell through the air, as Dad and the pilot wrestled Mom to the floor of the basket, Thorn leaped over the side, clutching at his clothes.

And then, midair. he shifted.

Not into his small shift. For the first time ever, he shifted into his large shift—a giant, bloodred dragon with jet-black talons the size of scimitars. With one powerful flap to propel him down, he dove for my plummeting body, then caught me with one outstretched foot. Zooming up into the sky, his wings stretched and pistoning us into the air, he dwarfed the balloon below us.

The power of a child in a dragon's body.

I gasped, breath restored.

"I knew it!" Dad roared from the balloon, his voice booming with laughter, as if this were a hilarious prank that had gone even better than expected. "I knew he could do it with a little motivation!" Dad clapped his hands to his knees, doubled over with mirth.

"You asshole." Mom shook her head. "You could have gotten them killed."

With a delicate thrust of his giant talons, he tossed me into the balloon and Mom's sobbing embrace. Moments later, the balloon lurched, pitching us all sideways, and we fell onto our backs, eyes skyward. Thorn had used his talons to grab on to the envelope, the sleeve of the balloon, puncturing it.

"Thorn, no," Mom yelled up at him, but talons just kept shredding the fabric.

Just as I opened my mouth to finally let out a scream, the basket jerked—upward.

My brother lifted us, holding the balloon in his feet, and our balloon ride continued. Not in the way he'd wanted, breathing fire up into the envelope, but with him as the pilot, controlling everything.

"You're going to pay for that envelope." The

pilot's teeth grated against each other. "No more fucking Signum," he muttered.

"So what can we do now, here, to help Iphigenia, if we can't bring her back?" Rhys asks, his question hauling me back from the difficult memory.

I press my hands together and offer my cousin a silent thank-you. "Well, what are our options if she's able to get the portal back open from the other side?"

Caspian raises his voice, the words coming out in a rush. "I can shift and jump in as my lion, tear this creature's face open. Shit, you can shift too, Dom, and help me. Two badasses, that demon won't stand a chance."

"We need him alive until we get Thorn back," says Rhys, the voice of reason. "And Iphi wouldn't want us killing anyone."

"That's true. She'd never forgive us." I sit down at the front of the line and look back at my brother and cousin. Singular. "Where's Nolan?"

Rhys and Cas exchange looks, jumping up to look for him. I remain seated in front of the tree in case the portal opens again, wrapping the rope around my midsection.

They both return after a few minutes, shaking their heads.

"He's gone," says Caspian.

I sigh. "I thought he was past this."

"Maybe he ran to get help," says Rhys.

"Or maybe he just ran," says Caspian.

I nod. "Old habits die hard."

"Dammit," growls his brother in a low rumble.

I stand up and hand the rope to Rhys. "He'll come back. He always does. Go ahead and wrap the rope around your waist too, Rhys, but Cas, you just hold on to the end."

"Why?"

"Just in case the portal reopens and we get pulled inside too. Otherwise, no one will know where we are."

Caspian nods, and a few minutes later, two of us are wrapped and sitting, holding the tension on our end.

Here with my pack, the sun hidden above the trees, the forest air cool even in the heat of the late summer, I'm able to dissect my fears. Ease into the sensations. Wear them. Taste them. Two members of my pack sit next to me, feeling the same exact emotions, no doubt.

We're all afraid for Iphi, we're all afraid for Thorn, and we all want Nolan to come back of his own volition.

But the overwhelming thought of losing our girl to this monstrous demon has me entertaining some terrifying thoughts. What does the Scrim want with her? Will Thorn be enough to stop him?

Iphigenia

The darkness is biting, like a sub-zero-degree weather front that you can't shake. One that crawls deep into your bones and makes a home there. A home that no fire or hot bath or warm blanket will ever warm.

One thing that does feel warm and familiar, though, is the sensation of rope in my hands. But as I'm about to climb up to loosen the weight on my waist, something small and furry climbs over my hands. I shriek and let go. As I dangle, again by my waist, I remind myself that many types of creatures could be living here, and if the Scrim is any indication, they all probably bite.

I gulp stale air and taste ash and debris on my tongue, then count to three and clutch the rope above me to pull myself up it for a foot lock, so that it no longer yanks on my spleen. All is silent in this place and the furry creature is gone. The Scrim, though not touching me, is close by. I can sense him.

What I really need right now is light. And poof, as if I'm an actual lantern, a light emanates from my body, casting a faint glow around me. In the dim light, the Scrim's massive face hovers a few yards in front of me. Wings! I would not have predicted that. A monster with wings. Like a dragon. Except, I remind myself, Thorn is no monster.

"Lady Iphigenia." He inclines his massive head. "So glad you could join me in my world. Now let's get down to business, shall we?"

"The only business I have with you is getting my friend back." I clutch the rope between my legs. Lucky for me, I can hold a foot lock for at least an hour. The nerves on the tops of both my feet are permanently numb from doing so all these years.

"Exactly. I'd like to proffer an exchange." He flies closer to me and I clench the rope tighter with my hands even as I lean my body away from him. "Your dragon boyfriend in exchange for your mother."

"My mother? But why?"

The beast rubs his humungous white hands together, the claws glistening as though wet from a fresh kill. "Ask *her* that, not me. Do we have a deal?"

"No!"

He opens his mouth, baring double rows of

razor-sharp fangs at me. "Very well then. Plan two. I keep you here and send word to her. She'll exchange herself for her favorite daughter, of that I'm sure." His laugh is maniacal, like an entire insane asylum filled with murderers all laughing at once.

I laugh too. Partly to disarm his menace but mostly because what he proposes is ludicrous. My mother, for all of her repressed love, would never sacrifice herself for one of her children. Or for anyone. Not anymore. "Good luck getting Aurelia to do anything that Aurelia doesn't want to do."

He stops laughing and tilts his head, like a bird of prey sizing up its next meal. "We'll see about that, witch."

I shrug as best I can while holding on to a rope in pure darkness. "Go ahead and try."

His smile is chilling and if I weren't already chilled to the bone, I'd either turn into a full-on icicle or explode. "Wait here." The beast chuckles, rising above me on mangled wings. They're dark and tattered, like the wings of a bat after it's survived a fight with an alley cat, but they serve their purpose.

I hold my breath until he disappears above me, drop my foot lock and start to climb.

CHAPTER FIVE

THORN

I stretch my wings, unsure of time here in Brae. A dull light from above highlights the burnt hull of this place. At least it's no longer pitch-black. The light is new. Is this what passes for sunrise in this hellhole?

"Did you sleep well?" Astra approaches me with her tiny hands held out.

I shift on the ashes that cover the ground. At least they make a soft bed. *What happened to this place?*

"The Scrim happened," Astra says with a sigh. Basil approaches and puts his arm around her waist.

The Scrim? The same one who tried to destroy the Edge a few years back? Must be. *How did he get into Brae?*

"He was born here," says Astra.

"One of us," Basil adds.

I stand up and shake off the ash. The two pixies fly up in the air to avoid the mess. *What happened to him?*

"A witch's curse." She shrugs.

He nods. "Unrequited love."

Around us, a brown fog hangs in the air. It's so thick that visibility is only a few feet in any direction. I don't know if there's a sun in this place or if it's tumbled from the sky. No plants or trees remain. Everything is blackened and cruel. And the smell—putrid, like rotting flesh left out in the sun for far too long.

What do you eat? Drink? This place looks . . . dead.

Basil clutches Astra's hand and then lands back on the ground in front of me. "Come." They walk into the gloom, into the brown sludge that is their atmosphere, and I follow.

"Our water supply has dried up and if we don't replenish it soon, the rest of our civilization will die." His voice is choked with grief.

What are you using now?

They lead me to an expansive area that looks like it used to be an ocean. Nothing remains but dried fragments of sea grass, polished glass, shells and lava rocks. Astra extends her arm to encompass the area. "This was our sea, where we drank and bathed."

Huh. Must have been a fresh-water ocean, unless the Smurfs like salt way more than humans do.

"It was also where the portals opened for travel between worlds," says Basil. "But no more."

I walk onto the dried seabed and breathe fire onto the rocks. Maybe there's water below them, like a well.

"We tried digging," he says, "but the spring has dried up."

Astra lets out a small sob. "It was supposed to be eternal."

You stored what you drilled?

"We did," she says, "but now we tap a tree, the only one left that hasn't been destroyed."

"Yet," Basil mutters.

"We try to bring liquid and food to the others. We spend the greater part of our day doing so." She takes flight, spreading her tiny gossamer wings like that of a dragonfly.

Where are they?

"We'll show you." Basil lifts off and I do as well, following my two new friends.

They start across the great desert expanse and Basil pulls up next to me. "Everyone is gathered together. There are outliers who remain hidden but the greater part of the flock is holed up in the old city, where we huddle together to keep warm and work together to make food and raise the children."

Why are you two alone?

"We spend time tapping the madapl tree. It happens to be close to our old house, so we fetch water when we can."

"When we near the city it may be a good idea for you to wait behind until we come get you." Astra approaches my other side. "If they see you, they may think you're another monster like the Scrim. We'll tell them about you first and then introduce you."

I understand. Tell me where.

They pull above me to confer and we fly for several more minutes before Basil says, "Here, Thorn."

I land on the rocky surface and begin pacing. I hate sitting idle.

"We'll be back to get you soon," says Astra and they fly away toward a thin line of smoke rising into the brown sky.

Rhys

I shift my weight and something moves in my periphery. The surface of the wood on the tree trunk changes, softening as the grain fluctuates. I jump to my feet and the others follow but we take wide stances and keep the rope taut.

"The portal is opening!" I yell and inwardly roll my eyes. *Way to state the obvious.*

The swirling of the portal comes faster and I step in front of Dominic. He lets me, even though he's the first one who has the rope around his belly.

"I've dealt with this demon before," I explain, knowing his first instinct is to protect me. But thankfully, Dom just nods, letting me take the lead here.

We collectively hold our breath, waiting for someone to pop out of the doorway. *Please be Iphi. Please be Iphi.* But when the whirlpool stretches wide and dissolves into a figure, it's the Scrim floating in the center. But he doesn't take a step out.

"Rhys," he smiles at me with gruesome teeth, "my prodigal puppet, how delightful to see you."

Instead of shrinking back, I raise my chin and take a step forward.

Dom presses his hand to the small of my back, letting me know he's got me.

Cas puts his hand on my shoulder and leans into

my ear. "If we do anything rash, our girl may be lost to us forever."

I toss my head, false courage surging as my family flanks me. "What do you want?"

The demon rubs his hands together and a wide smile splits his face. "I'm so glad you asked. You will fetch the girl's mother and exchange her for the girl."

I glance at Dominic, who shrugs and then nods. We've got to buy some time, regardless.

"Done," I respond.

"Wonderful, wonderful. I knew you'd all toss the witch into the inferno for your prize." A puzzled look spreads over his garish features and he turns to look over his shoulder. "Little girl, you have no idea what you're—" And then he roars in pain and disappears from sight.

Dom inches forward, keeping the rope taut, and everyone else inches forward with him.

A second later, Iphi's curls appear, a halo of light blazing around her head. Dominic leans forward and grabs her arms, the rest of us running in to help. As soon as we haul her small body through the gap, the door whirls shut.

She jumps up from the forest floor and pounds on it with her fists. "Thorn! No, Thorn!" Iphi crumples on the dry leaves and shakes her head, tears spilling down her cheeks.

Iphigenia

The men help untie the rope from my waist and Caspian helps them remove theirs. "I need to talk to my mother." I bite my lip and look back toward the tree. I should have stayed. I should have tried harder to keep the Scrim talking. But without an amulet . . . he'd have two hostages instead of just one. "We have to get Thorn out of there and we have to find Nolan."

"Nolan will turn up," says Rhys. "Going back in there is too dangerous. Open the portal for us. I'll go."

"What?" Dominic wraps the rope around his hand, trying to coil it. "So we can lose another sibling to the dark world?"

Rhys plucks the rope from Dom's shaking hands, who lets him. Rhys coils the rope using his hand and elbow. "Better me than Iphi."

"Hell yes, dude," Caspian says.

"Wait a minute, guys." I clear my throat. "Don't I get a say in this?"

I get a chorus of "No!" in response.

I look at Dominic. "Dom?" He's the one who always advocates for me to be my own person. He's the one who knows my secret. I send out little tendrils to probe but his mind is closed to me. That's a first.

I take a step toward him when something grabs me from behind. The smell of sewage invades my senses. "No struggle, pretty thing." A wet voice gurgles in my ear.

"Take your fucking hands off her." Rhys drops the rope and lunges.

The ghoul sidesteps him, holding me in front as a shield.

Rhys looks at me, a question in his raised brow.

I close my eyes and try to summon my magic, to free one more ghoul from the Scrim's influence, but I'm exhausted. I already used most of my energy to cure the six who attacked me at my performance hours ago—though I'm so tired it feels more like days ago—and then I used the rest to open that frigging portal. "Tapped," I whisper.

Almost in unison, Caspian and Dominic leap behind a tree, and then there's the sound of tearing flesh and breaking bones.

Another ghoul grabs Rhys from behind but he spins free and kicks it hard, in the face. The man falls down, dark blood gushing from his ruined nose.

"Was not wise to evade Master," says the one holding me. "Open the door or he'll open it for you."

Interesting. The ghouls can't open it by themselves? Well I can't right now either but even if I could, without a new amulet, it would be suicide and I can't do that to Thorn. "Of course. Just let me go so I can perform my magic." The ghoul releases me but stays so close he's practically my new shadow. I shuffle forward and start mumbling Latin. *"Amo, amas, amat . . ."*

It's gibberish, but it doesn't matter what I speak. I can't work any spells without re-juicing my power anyway.

Roars rent the air as both Caspian and Dom leap into the clearing.

The majesty of Dom as a black panther constricts my throat. I've never seen his large shift before but it's as though I've known what it was all along. And maybe I have. Beside the black panther, the king of jungle, Caspian in his lion shift. I stare at them with my mouth unhinged.

The ghoul behind me snuffles and makes a grab for my arms again, but Dominic's panther pounces. His lips are pulled taut over his large, intimidating fangs, but instead of ripping and shredding, he yanks the ghoul up by the scruff of his shirt like he's a wayward kitten. Dom pulls the ghoul deep into the forest, Caspian following with Rhys's attacker in his maw.

Rhys grabs my hand and we run toward the Grove, where, hopefully the ward still holds.

CHAPTER SIX

THORN

I've been pacing for what seems like forever, waiting for Astra and Basil to return, when a high-pitched whine punches my eardrum. I know I'm supposed to wait. My mistress was explicit in her instructions, but that sound . . . My mind is thick as though I've buried my entire head in mud, as though the sound has driven out every other sense in my body.

Another noise, a scream or a wail perhaps. My mistress may be in trouble and need my help. I lift off in search of the sound, my heart thumping hard against my chest. The wailing continues, beckoning, until I reach a large, rocky hill dotted with mounds of smaller stones. A small, hooded figure with a staff walks toward me, a hand dropping from its obscured face. Where is my mistress?

I sniff the air and her scent is not on it. Only this creature's, who is male and mortal. Where is my mistress? How dare this creature take me from her! Or did he take her from me? Rage compels me closer and I approach slowly, stalking my possible prey. He holds a hand out in front of his body, palm up, in a supplicating gesture.

"Please . . . help me," he rasps, pushing the hood off his head. It falls back to reveal a nightmarish face, blackened and burnt. The crust of a man. What happened to him?

The man's lips part to speak again but only a grating sound escapes, like sandpaper and grit. I mantle my wings and he takes several shaky steps back, but the fight has gone out of me. There's something familiar about him. And there's nothing threatening about this husk of a man.

Maybe he can hear my thoughts, like Astra and Basil. *Who are you?* I ask but he does not respond.

I take another step forward and he drops to the ground. "Please . . . just kill me," he wheezes. "I called you here to— I don't deserve to live. I don't want to live anymore. Just burn me up. I'm ready." With a throaty gasp, he raises his hands high above his head.

I rear up on my back legs and open my mouth to do as he asks. After all, I am a beast and this human could be here to hurt my mistress. And I've done it before, it's easy. But then a memory slams into me. A memory from my past? What past? Haven't I always been here? But there's no denying the radio fuzz.

In a flash I'm on a dirty, familiar New York street corner. I know it's the one on the Lower East Side near Tompkins Square, and I remember. I took our pack to that park to sleep in sometimes, Dom standing watch for the cops who swept through on a regular basis.

The end of summer in NYC, around September, the air was close to perfect. Not too hot during the day and not too cold at night. That night, there was a wind blowing in the scents from the East River and we all shifted to our smallest animals to run around the park together. The youngins wanted to play. I usually hid my shift. The others were all animals humans knew about, so if anybody caught sight of them, no one would go running and screaming to the cops. But not me. A dragon is difficult to explain, at least outside of the three enclaves on Earth where we can live out in the open.

New York City is not one of those places.

I flew up to perch in a tree, like always, out of sight of the screamers. Dom joined me in his owl shift. Caspian's gray fox shift, ever playful, climbed up a neighboring tree. It was early and I wasn't on high alert. I didn't see the drunken man enter the

park until it was too late. Although we rarely inter-
acted with humans, we all knew Ted and we all
knew to stay away from him. Ted was wearing his
signature filthy football cap, a battered red cardinal
on its brim. We used to make up stories about why
he wore a hat from an Arizona team, none of them
complimentary.

Dom and I had just started a game of chase and
were flying around in wide circles high above the
streetlamps, focusing on each other instead of our
brothers.

It wasn't until the screaming started that I dove
down for a closer look. Ted was holding a crack pipe
in one hand and Nolan in the other. He had our
packmate by his tail, swinging him in circles.

"You filthy, dirty scum," Ted slurred through
missing teeth. "Dirtier than me. Don't deserve to
live."

Without thinking, I swooped toward him. My
plan was to grab Nolan and carry him to safety but
the bastard was swinging the kid so hard his tail
broke off and he sailed through the air.

Pure rage clouded my vision. The feeling was so
potent, so much stronger than anything I'd ever felt
before. We'd all been threatened, of course.
Numerous times. But not like this. No one had ever

physically removed one of my cousin's limbs. I lost it.

I opened my mouth and roared. But it wasn't sound that came out.

It was a torrent of flame.

You were only sixteen and it was instinctual to protect us. I would have done the same thing, Caspian reminded me for the next ten years—until I clocked him in the face because he wouldn't stop bringing it up.

I believe Caspian, that it could have been any of us. If he'd been in his lion shift, he might have torn the guy apart. But he wasn't and he didn't.

This one was on me. All my fault. I knew better. I was a hormonal teen who'd neglected to practice my fire breath, believing myself invincible. No reason to tone it down. It was our secret weapon if we ever got cornered. I only used my fire breath for show—up until that fateful night, the night I burned a man alive.

Burned him to death.

As the memory fades and with it the sense of any other place and time than this one, a single thought remains: I was a killer, once. It was accidental, but that doesn't change the outcome. I never learned to forgive myself. Deep in my head, there's a faint, lovely voice telling me it wasn't my fault, but I can also see that burnt and charred face, so similar to the one that now stands in front of me.

But the other man didn't want to die and this one does. Does that make it all right? If I follow his wishes, I won't be a murderer, will I? What if I don't do it and he changes his mind and wants to live? Who am I to take the life of someone in duress? That doesn't feel like the right thing to do. No, I only take orders from one person now, and it's not this man. My mistress needs to decide what to do with this man.

I lift off and fly over the burnt man, hooking my talons through his robes. Rising with a screech, he flails below me as I fly toward the Nexus with him in my grasp.

Rhys

*I*t's times like these that I envy my cousins. They get to shift and fight for the woman we share, the woman we love. And I get to run. *You're running with her*, I remind myself as we head back to the Grove. I barrel up the steps to my tiny house, the Cliff, with Iphi in tow. I throw open my front door and fight not to physically push her inside. Then I follow, slamming and locking the door behind us. We collapse on the floor together in a heap, and she curls herself in my arms.

"Are you okay? What do you need?" I drop kisses on her forehead and hair and she pushes her body into me, shaking.

"That place . . ." she whispers. "I was barely in there but the smell, the darkness . . ." She shudders and I tighten my hold on her. "It's like it was a whole world of death and decay." She pushes herself against my chest and looks into my eyes. "We have to get Thorn out. Whatever it takes."

"Yes, of course. We will. I promise." I kiss her forehead again and then her cheeks. She sags against me and I hold her tightly until her breathing calms and she leans her entire weight against me. Asleep?

Some time later there's a knock on the door and we both startle.

"It's us," says Caspian and I leap up to unlock it for him.

Dominic and Cas stand naked on the stoop. Both are trembling, even in the warm summer air.

Iphi jumps up and goes to them, pulling them into her embrace, being the rock they need right now.

"Nolan?" she whispers and they shake their heads. She pulls back and looks each one up and down. "Are you hurt?"

"Scratched up a little but other than that . . ." Dominic cups her face and kisses her on the lips. "No big deal."

She darts her pink tongue out to taste the ghost of his kiss.

"Come inside. Both of you. Do you need anything to drink? Or eat?" I motion for them to enter and everyone does.

"What we need is a shower," says Caspian.

"Of course. You know where it is." I close the door behind them.

"You go first," Cas says to Dom. "You're stinkier."

Dom rolls his eyes. "That'd be a first." He gives Iphi a small smile and a wink, then turns and heads toward my bathroom.

Cas digs in my closet and throws on a robe while he waits for his turn in the shower.

Their forced cheer is obvious, but welcome. I know they're only doing it to distract Iphi—or maybe it's for all of us too. Thorn is lost, Nolan is lost, and we nearly lost Iphi.

Iphi sits on a barstool at the counter and I make everyone tea. Cas sits next to her and takes her hand in his.

"What happened to the ghouls?" She looks down at their clasped hands, drawing small circles on the back of his with her free one.

"We took them to the police station, actually. There's no way we're going to trust them not to come after you again. When you get your strength back, you can change them back."

She nods and I put a steaming mug of tea in front of her.

A wetter, cleaner Dominic walks into the living area wearing a towel and I hand him the cup of tea I made for myself.

"Thanks, Cuz." He takes it from me and blows on it.

Caspian slides off the stool. "My turn." He kisses Iphi on the top of her head and heads into the bathroom.

I wave Dominic toward my closet. "Feel free to borrow something." He turns toward it.

"Wait." Iphi's voice is a little breathless and she's eying him. "How 'bout we all go up to the loft and cuddle for an hour before you take me back to my mother's? We can wait for Caspian there."

Dom and I exchange glances, giving each other a *hell yes, bro* smile. I pick a giggling Iphi up and carry her toward the loft. Dominic drops his towel and clambers up, leaning over to help Iphi.

We lie down on either side of our girl and wait for her to make a move, if she wants to.

"It'd be a more comfortable cuddle if we were all naked," she says and I practically tear off my clothes in my hurry, throwing them over the side of the loft.

When I turn back, Dominic is removing hers slowly. As he unbuttons her blouse, he places kisses on each bare patch of revealed skin. She smiles at me, her eyes at half-mast, and I unbutton her jeans, following suit and placing kisses on each portion of bared skin.

She slides down deeper, burrowing into the bed, and lets out the moan I love to hear, the one I'd give my left nut to listen to for the rest of my days. I pull each long leg out of her jeans and kiss my way back up, licking and nipping her toned inner thighs, trailing my tongue along every, delicious inch of her. Every centimeter. Every millimeter. I can't get enough of Iphigenia. I can't taste enough of her, smell enough of her, see enough of her. She makes a little noise and I look up to find Dominic kissing her. His hand weaves around the back of her neck as he leans over, playing tongue hockey. I move back to the job at hand, running a finger over her flat belly and hooking it underneath the elastic band of her panties.

As I grab the thin cloth with my teeth, she lifts

her ass, allowing me to pull them off, though I make damn sure my fangs never graze her tender flesh. She groans into Dom's mouth and pushes her hips up. I lean in to smell her ambrosia. The light blond curls of her mound tickle my upper lip as I kiss her pubic bone, even gripping a small amount of hair in my teeth and tugging.

"Rhys!" She giggles and moves her hands to the back of my head before resuming her make-out session with Dom.

The scent of this woman is what I imagine heaven smells like, or what I'd want it to smell like if I had my choice. I wish I could bottle her scent and carry it with me to smell whenever the sun dipped behind a cloud, whenever someone cut me off in traffic, whenever my mood turned black. She's all honeysuckle and musk and I breathe her in as I part her pink lips and dip down for a taste. Her back arches when I plunge my tongue inside and Caspian's head emerges over the side of the loft, slamming me right back down to Earth.

"You started without me?" His voice is warm and he's smiling at the sight of our girl, naked and spread out before us like a platter of exotic fruit with enough for all to eat their fill. Caspian clambers up and leaps over everyone to join in from the other side. He fondles her breasts, sucking in one peaked, pink nipple before she pushes my head back down.

I want to make her come with my tongue and fingers while the others service her from above. Then I want to plunge my cock in her from behind while she services the both of them. One of my darkest fantasies about her, me and my brethren is triple penetration but I don't think she's quite ready for that. Especially not without talking about it first.

I swirl my tongue against her clit while slipping one finger, and then two, inside of her, curving them forward to press on her sweet spot. I know how to make my girl come quickly. I also know how to bring her to the edge but not let her pass over the precipice for a very long time. But tonight she needs the quick release. She's just been through hell and we need to take her mind off what she's lost.

Her moans turn into pants, which slip out around Dominic's mouth. She tugs at my hair with an insistence that means *stop fucking around and make me come*. So I add a third finger and curl them just a fraction of a centimeter more, flattening my tongue out along her clit. Iphigenia is a fan of the slow lick, as opposed to the quick flick, and I lengthen the strokes to cover above and below her swollen nub. Right before she's about to come, her clit swells just a fraction larger and her body releases the sweetest taste I've ever experienced. The moment is near and I change my long, languid licks to a firm suck, pulling her full, tight bud into my mouth as she releases. Our woman bucks and screams, her arms flying off my head. My cousins hold her down so I can keep teasing her with my tongue and fingers, pulling out the multiples we've all happily discovered. Her body vibrates and thrashes as I change my tongue speed and angle, now using tight, sharply pointed licks and grazing her with my fangs. My fingers continue to pump but I add the twist I know her body responds so well to. And before her second orgasm has receded, her third slams through her.

"Oh Rhys, yes, yes, fuck me with your hand," she wails and I admit, I love hearing her scream my name when she comes.

I dutifully pump in and out, placing my palm flat over her throbbing clit until her body collapses down and her breathing is no longer clipped. But there's no rest for this wicked witch. As soon as her body has normalized, I leap up and kiss her. Dominic sits back on his heels and Caspian waits too.

"Are you up for something a little different?" I growl into her ear.

"Yes." Her voice is soft and heavy.

"Can you sit up?"

She wobbles to her knees, Caspian helping her. I jut my chin toward the tiny nightstand I managed to fit in the space and he removes a condom from the drawer and hands it to me. *Gotta love bro speak.*

"I'm going to fuck you from behind now," I snarl. "And you're going to suck off my cousins, one by one. Understood?"

Dominic raises a brow at me. The sensitive one, he'd no doubt ask her if that was okay first. I know her well enough to know that if it wasn't, she'd say so.

"I'd love to," she purrs and I give Dom a smug smile.

"Men, take position," I order, quite liking this new role of mine.

Iphi shuffles to the side and Caspian moves next to Dominic but neither men look at each other; they're both staring at Iphigenia. I don't blame them. She's the looker here, and with her naked rump and swaying tits . . . I could shoot my wad without even touching her. I slap her ass and move my hand down between her thighs, rubbing her own slick juices against her clit. I hold the condom in my free hand and tear it open with my teeth, then roll it over my throbbing dick. Replacing my hand with my cock, I rub around her entrance, waking up all her nerves and getting her come all over me and the condom.

When I push into her tight little opening, she gasps and falls forward but I pull her back up by her shoulder. Caspian moves to one side of her and holds her up, leaning down to take her mouth. She groans into him, kissing my cousin for a few minutes while I bury my cock deep inside her.

As soon as I get my rhythm going, she stops kissing Cas and reaches out to grasp Dom's cock. Sitting on her knees she's not at the correct level so she leans forward, bracing herself with one hand. I wind my hands through her hair to help and she drops her mouth onto Dom's cock, sucking with vigor. That's our girl.

Caspian crouches down and I watch in amazement as she wraps her other hand around his stiffy, stroking him in time with her mouth over Dom's dick.

I close my eyes and concentrate on the walls of her pussy rolling and squeezing around my cock, then move my hand around underneath to strum her clit. She moans and grinds her ass back into me, pumping along my length. The harder I press, the more she pumps. When I open my eyes again, she's switched brothers. Now Caspian's in her mouth and Dom's in her hand. Their eyes are closed, heads back, but I leave mine wide open, focusing on the perfect quartet. It's like a flawlessly executed string of *kata* in aikido. This woman has offered herself to us body and soul, but we're not the ones in control. She's controlling us, controlling every single pleasure zone in every single man at once. It's a powerful performance—and why wouldn't it be? The woman is a consummate performer. But this act is one she'll never show anyone but her men. And like she's heard her cue, her pussy tightens even further, clamping down on my cock and pulling my orgasm out. The four of us wail together in utter ecstasy, Iphigenia coming all over my cock, me bursting inside of her, Caspian shooting down her throat and Dominic dirtying my clean sheets.

Ten minutes later we're all wrapped around Iphigenia, giving her the cuddle she more than deserves, the one she now needs. The one we all need.

CHAPTER SEVEN

IPHIGENIA

The men drop me off at Aurelia's house. They want to come inside but it's not a good idea. Not yet. I need to make nice, yet again.

They do get out of the car and I kiss each one of them—down the street, out of sight of any windows. Though that won't matter if Aurelia's feeling extra paranoid and has her crystal ball out. Of course, the lingering sexcapade we had earlier flies to the surface and I want to devour each one of them right here, out in the open, neighbors be damned. *Rein it in, sex kitten.*

"We're extra worried about you now." Caspian holds me around my waist and I wish he'd never let go. "You'll text?"

"Of course. And I'll see you all in the next day or two."

"Promise?" Dominic pets the back of my hair. "The ghouls are after you and we can't protect you while you're out of our sight."

"I'm sure Rhys won't let that happen." I move my gaze to his smoldering eyes and he winks in the moonlit night. Those eyes . . . those lips . . . that co—

Dominic kisses the top of my head. I wish he'd kiss something else. *Down girl, focus. Plenty of time for that later.*

"Good point." Caspian leans in to steal another from my mouth.

"We love you, Iphigenia Diantha Holt," says Rhys.

"I love you too. My heroes." I stand on tiptoe to kiss each one again, and they wait until I've walked down the street and opened Aurelia's door.

Luckily, my key works—Mom has a nasty habit of changing the locks when she's mad at her daughters—and I enter, shutting the door behind me with a soft click. In moments, Armageddon is winding his way between my legs, mewling.

"Iphigenia?" Mom calls from her bedroom.

"Yes, Mama. I'm sorry to wake you."

Mom and Alistair, her partner, pad into the foyer. He hugs me and Mom stands back, looking me up and down with a frosty chill.

"Did you forget something?" she asks.

"Now dearest," Alistair places his hand on her shoulder, "let's offer her some tea."

Mom sniffs and walks into the kitchen. We follow. She lights the hearth and places a teapot on it. I get some cups and pull some dried herbs from the rafters. "Mother, peppermint?" She sighs heavily in response and I add some to a cup.

A scratching at the window draws all our attention. Army jumps on the counter and hisses at Rhys, who is standing outside, meowing, in his housecat form.

"Botting!" Alistair rushes to the window to let him in. His grandfather still doesn't know the cat's his grandson, and though I've wanted to tell him, it would put him in a very awkward position with Aurelia. He'd have to make a choice whether to lie to her or nark on me. Plus, if my mother knew, there's no way she'd let him inside to sleep with me.

As soon as Botting enters, Army tries to attack but I hold him back. "There's enough love for both of you." I take my childhood cat in my arms and love him up. Rhys understands.

"How about I take Army into our bedroom?" asks Alistair, taking the cat from me.

"Thank you."

Once they leave, Mom and I sit at the kitchen table with Botting perched on the counter.

"Why are you home?"

Wow, just cut to the chase? "I need your help. I need a new amulet."

"Let me guess." She slides out her chair. "You gave yours away. Again." It's not a question.

I chew on my lower lip and look up at her through my lashes.

"How about this time you make it yourself? You're so quick to give them all away and I have no desire to make another one for your . . . friends. It's time you learned."

Wow! I suck in both of my lips to keep from showing a reaction. If she senses my excitement, hears the quick thrumming of my heart, she'll change her mind. "You'll teach me to make them?" My voice comes out a squeak.

For as long as I can remember, Aurelia has done her level best to keep her witchy daughters in ignorance. She only ever taught Chrys the basics, me a little more, and Sadie nothing at all. She discouraged us from experimenting and confined lessons to the simplest, least dangerous spells. I learned long ago to stop begging her for a peek in her grimoire—nothing was sure to send a stab of panicked worry through her faster. And now she's *volunteering* to teach me how to cast one of her most powerful, difficult, secret spells?

Her nostrils flare as though she's angry but she's not looking at me, she's looking past me, out the window. "Tomorrow morning, at dawn."

Botting meows.

"And lock that disgusting creature in your room."

"Yes, Mama. Thank you, Mama." I stand and move to kiss her but she bats me away.

"Don't 'yes, Mama' me, girl." She pushes her chair further from the table, takes a last sip of tea, gets up and storms out of the room. "If you're not here at dawn, the offer is off the table."

As soon as she's gone, Botting jumps into my lap and nuzzles my face.

"Thank you for being here."

He mewls and paws my lap.

I pat my shoulder and he leaps up to it. "Let's go to bed."

He pushes his whiskers against my cheek and mewls again.

*A*t dawn Rhys is still in his is cat form, which must mean he's able to control his shifting better. The last time he spent the night in my room, he changed back to his human form and Mom almost caught him in my bed.

"You stay here," I whisper. "If she sees you, she may not teach me."

He yawns, circles a spot on my pillow and lies back down.

As soon as I enter the kitchen, Mom glares at me, then thrusts her grimoire in front of me. "Find the correct spell for the protection amulet and read it aloud to me."

I flip through the pages of the thick book. Despite having her permission, the act still feels illicit. Why the sudden change of heart? Has Alistair softened her?

I'm supposed to be looking for the amulet spell, but I can't help skimming the contents while I flip pages. When will I ever get the chance to look in it again? A hair regrowth spell, a bad luck spell, a spell to hex the third son of every fourth daughter with impotence—what on earth is that about?

A spell to open a portal.

But I don't have time to wonder why she has this particular spell in her grimoire or what it means. I make a mental note of the page number and keep flip-ping until I find the spell for the protection amulet.

Mom gathers the herbs as I read what's needed. It's a formality, since she's teaching me what to do, though I don't realize that until I peek over and see she's pulled down some High John the Conqueror root from the rafters before I even get to that line in the ingredient list.

"And most important, as you know, is the oil of abramelin. The spell won't work without that." She opens the cabinet and takes out a large amber glass bottle. "Light the fire under the cauldron now and then cast the circle."

This, too, is for me. Mom's powers are strong enough that she doesn't need to cast a circle for her spells to work, but for both of us to be working side by side, the space must be sacred and cleansed.

I light the fire under the cauldron and gather the candles for the circle. Mom separates the herbs and adds just the right pinch of this and pour of that into the cauldron as it heats. This part is new to me. She can add the ingredients before the circle is cast? I wonder for the second time if the circle is merely a formality to keep me occupied. Like the man behind the curtain—look the other way while I pull the levers. My mental tendrils licking out, I don't sense deceit, more like forced formality and something else. Ah yes, this is what other witches have to do, not my mother—so she is going through the redundant motions to teach me.

"Hail, guardians of the watchtowers of the east,

powers of air, golden eagle of dawn, star seeker, rising sun. Come!"

She repeats the incantation for all four directions and I echo each one after her.

When the candles are all lit and the circle is complete, I move next to her as she stirs the now-simmering herbs and oils, which turn a dark, liquid brown the color of Armageddon's eyes when he's intent on cornering his prey.

That's when I remember I have no amulet for her to add the herbs to and I start to hiccough.

"What is it, girl?" Mom narrows her eyes at me. "Use your words."

What she's really thinking is very different though, and I catch the flash of remembrance from when I was a little girl, new to this world, always clutching her leg like an unwanted burden.

After she tried unsuccessfully for the umpteenth time to peel me away and I clung even harder, she finally crouched down to my level, holding my gaze with her own. One warm brown eye the same color as Papa's, one cold blue eye reaching out to snare me in its web.

"You, Iphigenia, are the only one in this family who can hold us all together. This is your job and the most important one of all your sisters'. You are the strong one. You are the glue of the family, the one who will remain at my side always, the one who will bend your sisters to our will and always make your mama and your papa proud. It is your fate. There is no way around this and so you must promise me that always, you will live up to what the Goddess has chosen for you."

"I promise, Mama," I squealed, so proud that I was special in her eyes. The gift she gave me that became my curse. My ball and chain. An expectation I lived my entire life trying to fulfill but now doubt I ever can.

Mom clears her throat. A silver filigree amulet swings in front of my face, its chain wrapped around my mother's hand. She reaches out with her other one and pats my hair. It's a gesture that another mother might use to console, but I startle, not used to any physicality from her. I reach for the amulet but she yanks it away and moves to hold it over the cauldron.

"It's beautiful, Mama. Thank you."

Her shoulders soften. "I know you too well, my daughter. But this one I'm spelling so it will be impossible for you to remove when you find another stray you believe only you can save."

Rhys

When Iphigenia finally returns to her room, where I've paced a groove in the floor, she is red, her face the color of strawberry ice cream melting in the sun.

I run to her, wending my way around her legs, and as soon as she closes the door and sits down on the edge of her bed, I leap into her lap, looking up into those bright-blue eyes. They're the color of hope, of sunlight glistening and sparkling off the surface of a calm tide pool. The essence of starlight. "Meow."

She points to the sterling amulet adorning her slim neck, its silver filigree more elaborate and finely detailed than anything I've ever seen.

"Mama knew I'd give mine away again." She fingers the piece. It rests in the hollow between her clavicle and sternum as though it has taken up residence there, taunting me with its proximity to her softest bits. "She had this one already waiting for me."

"Meow." It's all I can say and somehow it's enough.

"I won't be able to remove this one though. Like my brand, it's here to stay."

I rub against her elbow and purr.

"Unless someone beheads me, of course." The tinkling of her laughter is in complete contrast to her words, making light of her fears instead of owning them. She glosses and glides over her true feelings in order to make others feel better, as if she can somehow control our emotions with her laughter.

I hiss, drawing her attention back to me. She looks down with raised brows and an open mouth.

"It was a joke."

I use every ounce of self-control not to hiss again.

She crumbles then, lying back on the bed and gathering me onto her chest. "You're right." Her voice is so soft, I can't have heard her correctly. "I cover up my true feelings."

How the hell did she know what I was thinking? Or was it an educated guess?

She lies silent for a long time, just petting me. Then she shifts me to her lap and sits up, rummaging in her cleavage to pull out several sheets of old parchment.

"My mother will kill me if she finds out I stole these." She opens them up and studies them.

What are they? I paw at one sheet, trying to draw it closer.

"Not now, Botting."

Not now? What the hell does that mean? She won't let me see them, holding them high and away from me. The hairs along my spine stand up, rising like a tiny magnetic airstrip. Were I in my human form, I'd have a hard time not snatching the papers away from her. I'll just have to trust that if I give her the time and space she's demanding, she'll show them to me when she's ready.

CHAPTER EIGHT

THORN

"There he is." Scanning the sky, Astra hovers with Basil directly above the rocky clearing where they left me.

I place the burnt man down below them on the bed of granite and silt. He stumbles before righting himself.

"You brought back the demon's assistant?" Astra shrieks.

"His aide!" Basil buzzes, darting around my head.

This man was a hostage. The monster kept him, like a pet.

"And you know this how?" hisses Basil.

Look. He's a shell being used as evil's servant.

The man stumbles again and then sits down hard, dropping his head into his hands. "Kill me, please."

His words are muffled, gravelly and wet. "Set me free from the slavery of the beast."

See?

"He could easily be lying," says Basil, "so we'll let our guard down."

"Where is the Scrim now?" asks Astra, scanning the horizon.

"He won't follow," says the man. "He can't get this close to your place of refuge."

"It's true, the sorcerers have surrounded the sanctuary with runes." Astra descends but stays just out of arm's reach.

The man looks up, his face wet with tears that have smeared some of the black soot that I thought were burns. It's ash. His face is blackened with ash. Fierce blue eyes pierce like a lance, straight to my heart. He wears eyes so familiar I'm sure I've seen them elsewhere. But no memory surfaces.

Can he enter the sanctuary? I ask my mistress.

She shrugs and Basil darts down, close to the man's face. He doesn't move to swat the pixie away. "I hope not."

The man doesn't react to my question. Yet again, he seems unable to hear my thoughts. He could be pretending, but . . . no. Something about this man screams broken, not scheming.

"What's your name?" asks Astra.

"Taylor," he responds. "My name is Taylor."

"Well, Taylor, let's see what happens when you approach our refuge." She darts ahead, glancing back at Basil before continuing.

He grumbles and shakes his head, then follows his mate.

I hover above my bedraggled quarry and open and close my talons, hoping he'll understand the meaning. He does and stands, positioning himself below me and bowing his head.

"Thank you for trusting me. I won't hurt anyone if left to my own free will."

I wrap careful claws around his shoulders and lift him into the air.

Dominic

It's been two days and neither Cas nor I have heard a word from Nolan. Thankfully, Rhys checked in yesterday and gave us a status update on Iphi. At least he'll call if anything changes.

Nolan and Thorn are the worry now. I have to believe that Thorn can protect himself until we find a way to get him out of Brae, but what about Nolan? With no word or sign of him, and no scent trail leading out of the forest, I'm beginning to think he hasn't run off after all. Could he have slipped into the open portal somehow when Iphi did? Is it wrong of me to hope that he's there too and that Thorn finds him?

Nolan's been running away since he turned fourteen, but I want to believe he's changed, even though I know from study and experience that people generally don't.

Maybe Nolan first learned to defy instructions from Thorn. Maybe his independent streak was my doing. Or maybe he learned to run away from Caspian. It was his initial introduction to us, after all, when Cas ran away from our pack on that bittersweet day our cousins came to live with us.

Thorn, all of sixteen at the time, stood at a pay phone in Central Park, shivering. Snow was falling and the ground was dusted a fine white. The only thing protecting him from the elements was a small cover over the top of the phone booth. He held on to the receiver so tightly I thought his hand would break.

"What the hell, Carter? Put your mother on the line. Now."

Carter was eight at the time, six years younger

than me. Thorn waited, jumping up and down to keep warm. Caspian and I huddled together next to him.

It was one of the many times I mourned the end of phone booths. The last one in Manhattan at Sixth and Fifty-Seventh had been a sanctuary for us many times. Two could pile inside at a time, taking shelter from the raging wind and snow when the subway was overrun by cops or gangs.

Thorn cleared his throat and I put my hand on Caspian's shoulder. "Clench your jaw so your teeth stop chattering, I wanna hear this," I said in his ear.

"Hello, Nora." Thorn's voice was clipped, angry and who could blame him? She'd refused to take us in, refused to help us. Sure, we were the children of her husband's other wife's sister but still . . . we were just kids. Abandoned kids at that.

Thorn listened for a few minutes and then started yelling. His voice was shaking and angry in a way I'd never heard before. It was straight out of *Godzilla vs. Mechagodzilla*, which we had seen the year prior by sneaking into a movie theater on a rainy day. Not to mention Thorn was using some very bad words—words that Caspian was forbidden to say. His eyes grew large before he broke free of me and took off down the icy pathway, veering away toward the snow-covered grass and into a cluster of trees.

I ran after him, calling his name, but the kid was fast, zigzagging through the trees until I lost him. He hid from us for the entire day, a day we spent looking for him everywhere we could think of. We checked our old squats and group hiding places, praying that he'd take to heart what Thorn had taught us and keep out of sight so the authorities wouldn't find him and turn him over to CPS.

Thorn insisted that I wait for Cas all day at the Washington Square Arch. It was our meeting area, the one place we all went if anyone got separated. Several hours later Thorn returned with our new brood. Welcomed by the absence of my youngest brother and a murder of squawking crows, Rhys and Nolan appeared in my life that frigid and snow-driven winter day.

Poor little Rhys clung to me the moment he saw me, probably because Thorn's arms were full of five-year-old Nolan and a garbage bag. If I hadn't been living on the streets with nothing to call my own, that green plastic bag evil Nora had stuffed with my cousin's sparse belongings would have seemed incongruous and cruel instead of normal.

"When can we go home and eat?" Nolan wailed from Thorn's arms.

Rhys, all of seven at the time, clung to my side, chewing his lip and shivering in a thin cotton jacket. I wrapped my arms around him as best I could, wishing Caspian would return.

Thorn turned to me, shielding his eyes from the sun's last hurrah. "If Caspian doesn't appear in the next hour, we'll have to take the kids somewhere warmer and come back tomorrow."

There was no way I'd agree to that but I kept my mouth shut, and even though I didn't believe in praying, I dropped a few that evening.

Right before the orange globe of the sun blinked out, Caspian finally approached, his head hanging low and his hands buried deep in his pockets.

It was difficult for Rhys and Nolan, losing their mother and being abandoned by their father. They were crossbreed vampires thrown into an already tight-knit family of shifters. Maybe it was because Cas and Rhys were just a year apart that they bonded like true blood brothers. Maybe it was because Nolan was so much younger than all of us. Or maybe it was because he always blamed himself for his mother's death. Whatever the reason, Nolan always chose to remain on the fringe.

My thoughts have gotten downright maudlin. Time for a distraction. I leave my house and rap on Caspian's round, red front door.

"Come on in," he says, "it's unlocked."

I pull the handle and it swings outward.

Peeking my head inside, the warm smell of coffee seizes me, tickling my nose and heightening my senses.

"Hey, man." Cas looks up from the stove. "I'm making Turkish coffee. Want some?"

"Do psychiatrists wear nerdy spectacles? Hell yes."

Cas shakes the weird pot with the coffee in it and peeks inside again.

"Why Turkish coffee?"

"Don't give me shit. I'm trying to take my mind off the fact that our brother and our cousin are missing."

So I'm not the only one in need of a distraction. "Yeah, about that." I cross to the sturdy wooden kitchen table. His hobbit house has a completely open floor plan.

"What about it?" He gives me his back.

"What if Nolan got sucked through the portal like Iphigenia, except he never made it out?"

Caspian slams the weird pot down on the stove and turns around, nostrils flaring. "And you only decided to mention that now? How the hell do you know anyway?"

I flash a tight-lipped, fake smile and modulate my

speech. "I tracked his scent. I found his crumpled clothing buried under a small boulder, so he must have shifted, but the scent trail doesn't go any farther than the clearing with the portal in it."

"Well shit, man." Cas, a lover of rituals, turns his attention back to the small pot, pouring me a tiny cup and then handing it to me.

I take a sip. It's strong. Almost too strong and I grimace, scrunching up my nose. Good thing Caspian's back is turned. I don't want to be rude.

"Fine, let's say he is. Either way, we know Thorn is there and we're not leaving him." Cas pours his own cup.

"Of course not. But the portal is closed."

"What if we asked a ghoul to contact the Scrim, get him to open it from the other side?" He swirls the coffee without drinking it.

"Maybe. There're some in a holding cell at the station. Sheldon wanted to see if Iphi could cast another spell like she did last time and turn them all back to normal, but now that Iphi's back at her mom's, Aurelia's stonewalling Sheldon. But why would the Scrim jump to do our bidding?"

"Good question." Caspian takes a sip of his coffee —and spits it out in the sink. "Oh shit, man. This coffee tastes like ass." He looks over at me. "You're drinking it?"

I shake my head and point to the cup on the tabletop, barely touched.

"So much for following the directions." He grabs my cup and his, dumping them both in the sink and covering them with water. "Thanks for being a sport."

"You're my brother. It's my job to support both your successes and your failures."

He snorts. "Does Aurelia think her daughter is safer with the ghouls in custody? And what about the station itself? Is it still protected under that ward she cast?"

"Not if the one at the circus already wore off."

Caspian nods, then turns to a cabinet. "Just great. Hey, man, I've been meaning to ask you something."

"Shoot." I pull out a stool and sit down.

"Sometimes it seems like Iphigenia's reading my mind." Caspian pulls down two clean glasses and pours us each a cup of water.

I stiffen. Shit. She asked me to protect her secret but it's only a matter of time before the others figure it out. "She's highly intuitive."

My brother goes to the fridge, rummages inside and returns empty-handed. "It's more than that." He levels his gaze with mine. "There's something you know that you're not telling me. I know that for sure. What I don't know, is why."

Iphigenia

*L*oaded with the spell I tore from my mother's grimoire, the amulet she made me and a skein of silks looped around one arm, I slip into the forest behind the Grove.

I had to wait an extra day for my men to go to work and to convince Mom to lock "Botting" in the windowless laundry room. I'm not proud that I had to lie to her. I told her I was terrified Army would rip him to shreds if he was wandering around the house and made up a story about him almost breaking my bedroom window to get at a bird; hence the laundry room prison.

Rhys was not happy but I told him it was for his own good. Then I told him I was going out to meet my sisters, assuring him I was safe with my amulet. Lying to the tiny chimera with the bicolored eyes was the last thing I wanted to do.

There's no way the men would let me go without them, but there is no way I am taking more of them into Brae, not with Thorn already stuck there.

I group texted Caspian and Dominic, assuring

them I was fine and just very busy and asking about their schedules, which is how I learned that tonight, they are both at work.

Last time I was here I marked the correct tree when no one was looking. It won't be easy to find it again but with a compass and the general direction, I have to believe I can.

For once, luck is on my side, because not only do I get away from the guys, but I also don't run into any ghouls bumbling around in the forest. Thank the Goddess for small favors.

After much less time than I expected, I find myself once again standing before the right tree. I pull the stolen sheets of the grimoire from my pocket and read the instructions.

With one hand resting on the gnarled wood, I recite the Latin aloud. *"Hoc apertum est portal ad alium se orbem terrarum, non nostra modo. Hoc nomen* Brae.*"*

A magical implement is required to trace symbols in the air, and I use my amulet to do so. A shimmer appears on the gnarled trunk, growing in intensity as my voice rises. The wood glows red and a moment later it spins counterclockwise, first as slow as the sand falling from an hourglass, and then in earnest. Yellow and blue sparks appear, one landing on my nose. I startle but it doesn't burn, so at least there's no chance of a forest fire. The wind picks up around me, whipping my hair and sweat-shirt, rustling the leaves and swaying the branches of the large oak.

Soon the spinning circle grows wider and then, it opens. I don't dare stop my recitation even though my hand pushes through to the other side. I'm about to pull back to get my bearing when the amulet grows hot and yanks right out of my hand—

Pulling me with it.

I jolt through the hole and tumble down, down, down. Without the silks to hold on to, I'm freefalling.

Something acrid burns my nostrils and my hair whips around my face, lashing against my cheeks and eyes. I squeeze them shut against the onslaught. The dull wind rushes by with no time for contem-plation.

I turn myself midair so I'm no longer tumbling headfirst and force my eyes open. Above me, the dying light from the hole is quickly fading out of sight. I should be scared, but a dull light surrounds me from below, pulling my attention downward. I land with a soft thud in what feels like a pile of dried leaves but, I soon discover with a sneeze, is actually ash. The fall was far but the drop wasn't painful, thanks to the piles of ash that broke my fall better than an aerobics mat.

Standing, I survey the landscape, though I can't see very far. In front of me is a tall brown tower. Squinting, I correct my initial inspection; it's more of a beehive daubed with mud and leaves. Tiny dark holes pepper the structure, and as I watch, a variety of bugs fly out of the holes, gathering en masse and heading straight toward me like a very dark, very angry tornado.

I duck, wrapping my arms over my head as the large bugs swarm over me. They buzz by my ears and into my hair. Sharp beaks and stingers burn my arms. Something chitters with gnashing teeth and the bugs stop their attack at once, launching up as though called away by their queen bee. I make a slit between my arms and peer out.

A large gray rat stands in front of me, and behind it, the bugs hover in the air. Except that they're not bugs, they're tiny people. A dozen of them at least, all holding tiny, pointed sticks blackened and twisted.

The rat chitters again and the swarm backs farther away but doesn't leave.

The rat is keeping them from attacking me. I stretch my hand down toward it and it runs onto my palm and up my arm, perching atop a shoulder and squeaking in my ear. I giggle at the tickle of its whiskers and turn to kiss its little face, a reaction I couldn't curb even if I wanted to.

The tiny creatures whisper among themselves, swarming together closer to my face.

"Hello," I say, addressing the swarm. "My name is Iphigenia Holt and I'm not here to hurt you."

"Iphigenia?" a little girl says and veers away from the swarm.

"Tansy, you get back here right now!" another calls, her tone frantic.

The girl obediently flies back to what I'm betting is her mother.

I stand with the rat still perched on my shoulder and brush my hands over the thighs of my jeans to wipe the ash away. "I'm here to find a friend. His name is Thorn, and he's most likely stuck as a dragon."

"How would she know that if it weren't true?" asks Tansy.

"Perhaps she's a witch and saw it in her crystal ball," says her mother. "Besides, isn't she the one the Scrim seeks? We give her to him and he'll give us back our world."

After that, the tiny creatures explode in a twittering so tumultuous I can't tell what's being said. The din escalates as they advance on me, faces red with rage. Some shake fists while others point their tiny handmade weapons, sharp and unfriendly. I take a step back and let out a yelp as something tugs at my hair from behind.

I'm surrounded by a large herd of angry, intimidating fairies. I hold up my hands and a spiked prong grazes it. Jumping back, I lose my balance and fall to the ground, the rat leaping off my shoulder. The tiny creatures swarm my chest, buzzing around me, some landing right on top of me, sharp sticks pointed directly at my watering eyes.

CHAPTER NINE

CASPIAN

*S*itting at my desk at the station, I push papers around, trying to look busy. I open and close a sketchbook and fumble through a folder of drawings and photos, unable to concentrate on them. Aurelia stopped by earlier with Alistair and cast a spell over the ghoul holding cell but nothing changed.

"I just do not understand *how* Iphigenia was able to transform them back into humans and I cannot," I overheard her saying to Alistair. "I'm stronger, older and smarter. They must have the events mistaken."

"Now, darling," Alistair patted her arm, "why not just ask her?"

Aurelia snorted and stormed out of the station with her boyfriend trailing after her like a well-trained dog.

How did Iphigenia do it? I saw it happen with my own eyes and suspect it has something to do with the "intuition" Dominic won't talk about. There's more to all of this than either of them is telling me, and as one of her boyfriends, I don't like it. Why should I be kept in the dark? Why should any of us? I wanted to see her today and ask her but she texted, saying she was busy trying to find a way to get us all into Brae to rescue Thorn. I haven't gotten the chance to tell her yet about what we think happened to Nolan, but at least he and Thorn probably have each other.

"Do you think Iphi is all right?" Dominic appears at my elbow in the break room. I didn't even hear him enter.

"Why? Do you think something is wrong?" I look up from the cup of coffee I just poured myself.

"I don't know." Dom rubs his hands together. "We haven't seen her in four days. I think something's wrong."

"Rhys is watching her." I add some milk and stir. "And she has her protection amulet."

"At least."

"Boys?" Sheldon approaches and we stand apart to make room for him.

"Sir." I offer him my cup of coffee to be polite but he shakes his head.

"We can't hold the ghouls here indefinitely. We need your girl to transform them back, like she did with the last group. Can you bring her down to the station?"

"Of course." Dom pulls out his phone and texts Iphigenia. "Why didn't you ask earlier?"

"We were interrogating them but they won't give anything up. Her mother was certain she could help, and she was adamant about not involving her daughter, but we've exhausted those avenues now." He twirls his gray mustache. "We need Iphigenia. She seems to be the only one who can truly save these creatures."

They're not the only things that she can save.

Iphigenia

I squeeze my eyes shut and send out a tendril of my empathic gift but it's dampened here, like a wet cloth dousing a flame. I pick up only that they're afraid, like me, but are they killers too? I have nothing to lose if they are.

"Please . . ." I whisper. "I'm only here to help."

The rat lets out a long, loud hiss, halting all argument. The weight from my chest lifts a moment later as they take flight and I crack open an eye, then sit up. The air fills with hissing, squeaking and chattering.

As though he's a rat king and they are his subjects, he addresses them. In rat speak. After another minute he climbs up my arm, through my hair and onto my head, where he continues talking.

"He's right," says a rotund fairy. "We bring Thorn to her and let him decide her fate."

Thorn? He's here and he's safe! I want to leap up and dance in the dust but instead I force myself to remain still, biting the inside of my cheek to keep silent.

"Why Thorn? He's new here too," says a smaller fairy. "We should bring Bagaata. As the ruling sorceress, she will decide."

"Why not both, Pappy?" says Tansy. "They can each make their case and then we vote, as always. It is the pixie way."

Pixies, not fairies. I vote for Tansy's choice but it doesn't look like I get to decide my own fate.

The rat chitters again from atop my head.

"Quiet, Wren speaks," says Tansy's father. Some fly closer to listen.

After the rat finishes, Tansy's father clears his

throat, "And so it's decided: we leave Wren here to watch the girl until we bring back the dragon and Bagaata."

Without further discussion, they turn as one swarm and fly away toward a horizon brown with silt.

As soon as they're out of sight, the rat climbs down my shoulder and arm and stops to sit on my outstretched hand. He chitters and twitches his whiskers at me. I'm completely unable to read the mind of the rat but I bring my face down close to him and smile. He continues chittering and runs in a circle on my palm as though trying to tell me something.

"I'm sorry, I don't understand what you're saying."

He jumps off my palm down onto the hard-caked ground, then spins and jumps. I shake my head, frowning. He stands on his two hind legs and grabs his tail with his front paws, waving it in the air like a conductor.

"Well you're obviously sentient. How about we play the *one for yes, two for no* game?"

He squeaks and flips his tail once.

"Do you understand me?"

One tail flip.

"Are you a pixie?"

Two tail flips.

"Do you know me?"

One flip.

After several minutes we've established that the rat is from Earth, not the world of the pixies. He knows both Thorn and me are from Earth as well. He is also a shifter stuck in his shift, like Thorn. He doesn't know why the pixies have chosen him to be their mascot but they trust him, and for some unknown reason, so do I.

Here's hoping this Bagaata is equally friendly—and that Thorn, wherever he is, is okay.

CHAPTER TEN

RHYS

*a*fter an entire day in this fresh-scented dungeon, one thing is clear: I've been hoodwinked. I'm so angry with myself that all I can do is shift back into my human form and pound on the laundry room door.

Luckily, some clothes have been forgotten in the dryer. Unluckily, they're all Aurelia's and the only thing that fits me is a housecoat. It's anything but flattering and I fear her response to me wearing her clothing more than her reaction to me being here at all.

For several hours no one responds to my pounding but eventually there's the click of a lock being turned and then the knob. Aurelia throws the door open and I jump back, almost burned by her rage.

"What the hell are you doing here?" she hisses.

Alistair is behind her. And while her eyes are as sharp as throwing stars, his are as wide as flying saucers.

"Rhys?" He takes a step toward me but Aurelia throws up an arm, holding him back. *"You're* Botting?" The deep pain in his gray eyes is like a punch to the gut. When I'm flattened like a fly against the washing machine, I realize that Aurelia must have used her magic. To *actually* punch me.

"Aury, stop. That's my grandson." He rushes forward and tucks an arm underneath my neck. "Come, son, let me help you out to the living room."

"Not in my dress." Aurelia's voice is deep, low and angry.

"Not now. This is not the time. Your dress can be rewashed."

Who cares about her fucking dress? "Where is Iphigenia?" I let Grandfather move with me to the couch while I catch my breath.

"What do you mean?" asks Aurelia, turning to Alastair. "What does he mean?"

But before he can answer, she breaks away from us, running to Iphi's room, where she flings open the door.

"Iphigenia!" she calls out but there's no response.

"We have to find her," I say. "She said she was going to her sister's."

Her mother appears in the doorway, her face ashen, a phone in her hand. "She's not answering her phone. Call the girls," she says to Alistair and hands him a phone.

Alistair calls Sadie and then Chrys, talking to each one briefly before shaking his head and dropping the phone in his lap. "She hasn't been to see either one of them."

"Try Dominic and Caspian." My mouth is dry.

Alistair hands the phone to me. I call both of them but it goes straight to voice mail. I try the police station, and the front desk patches me through to Cas. After a quick conversation, I hang up the phone and try the circus. Serlon hasn't heard from her in days. She was supposed to come in and train earlier but never showed.

I turn back to her mother, who is worrying her hands so fast she may take flight. "No one's seen her. What now?"

Iphigenia

*T*he rat and I curl up together on the hard ground to wait for Thorn. I need to talk to the sorceress, get some herbs and try to cast some spells here. If I can figure out what made the Scrim or how he entered their world, maybe I can banish him.

The little rat is curled in my arms when I'm startled by the whoosh of flapping wings. I sit up and scramble backward with the rat in my lap but I barely make it a few feet before the dragon tackles me.

"Thorn!" My cry is muffled underneath his bulk.

But instead of kissing me, he's holding me down and baring large, sharp fangs in my face.

"Thorn, stop. What's the matter with you? It's me, Iphigenia."

The dragon lifts his head to the sky and roars. Hot flames shoot from his mouth and brighten the dank, stale air. What the hell? Did the fall into Brae turn him completely dragon? Without time to worry about what happened, I shoot my arms over my head in submission. The dragon, mollified, looks around at the prattling pixies as a female approaches. She's wearing rags, like the others, and though her features are unique, she's indistinguishable from the rest of the pixies. Yet Thorn watches her as if she is the center of his universe.

"Thorn," her voice is high and authoritative, "don't hurt the human . . . yet."

His pupils form slits and he narrows his dark eyes at her, easing up on my chest.

The rat, which was thrown aside when Thorn landed on me, approaches the dragon and chitters.

Thorn stops and looks at me, blinking. Then he looks at the rat and bends to grab it with his maw.

"No," I cry and reach for the rodent, but Thorn has carefully picked it up and placed it on my chest.

The vermin chitters and waves a paw at Thorn. He blinks at it and tosses his scaled head.

The pixie woman clears her throat, flying closer to me.

"Thorn, off the girl," she commands and I clench my jaw. Does she have some sort of power over him or is she just crazy bossy?

He does as she says and leaps off me, leaving the rat, who clambers upon my shoulder as I sit up.

A male pixie follows the female one and I extend my hand, holding it out flat, palm up. They both land on it.

"Iphigenia, I'm Astra and this is my husband, Basil. Thorn has some . . ." She glances at Basil but he looks down at his hands. "Memory issues."

The rat makes a noise but Astra shoots him a look and he quiets.

"Did he remember anything when he got here?" I don't know why I'm even asking this. It's not like she'd know; he can't speak. But maybe, like the rat, the pixies can understand animals. And if they can understand them—what if they can control them too?

"No matter." She takes flight with her husband when another pixie flies down close to my face, buzzing around me like an angry fly. The newcomer wears dark robes and tiny jewels, and her hair is swept up on top of her head in an elaborate knot. After circling me twice she hovers directly in front of my eyes without showing any fear. She reminds me of my mother and I like her immediately.

"Hello." I blink and smile. "You must be Bagaata."

"Smart girl." Her voice is deeper than the others' but still high-pitched to my ears. "Are you here to help us or to help him—he who would destroy?"

"I am here to help you *and* him."

The pixies erupt in loud, angry catcalling, misunderstanding me, but she shushes them.

"No, not *him* him. Him," I say, pointing at Thorn.

"What do you mean, human?"

"My first priority is to help my friends. But if I

can, I'd like to help you and your land too. It wasn't always a ruin, was it?"

Bagaata tosses her head. Her gossamer wings buzz like a firefly's.

"The Scrim must be miserable to wreak such havoc on your world. Why has he done this?"

"He was once one of us," says Astra, flitting above me. "But he was cursed by a witch. After everything he's done to us, to our world . . ."

"We wish to destroy him." The buzzing of Bagaata's wings increase.

No point in arguing with them. I understand their anger even if hate only begets hate. "First things first. Do you have herbs, gemstones and fire I may use?"

"For what?" She darts to the left and then to the right.

"A spell."

"What kind of spell?" Bagaata flies closer to my face. "Don't you think we've used our own magic on that monster? It won't work."

The rat jumps up and down on my shoulder, then climbs back to the top of my head and chitters.

"No, Wren, we won't let the witch try," Bagaata says but Wren keeps speaking. Bagaata looks at Astra. "Silence him."

The small pixie produces a wand from the waistband of her ragged skirt. She points it at Wren but he runs down my back and burrows under me.

"Hey, what's going on?" I scoop up the rat, close my palms over him and stand.

"None of your concern. Now open your hands." Bagaata buzzes my head. "Astra, do it."

"Stop," I shriek. "Is this what you did to Thorn?" I level my gaze at Astra, who is glaring at my palms.

"What's it to you?" she replies, telling me everything I need to know.

"Besides the fact that Thorn is my friend? There's absolutely nothing about controlling another sentient being and stealing their free will that's okay. Nothing! You're no different than the Scrim!"

"Excuse me?" Astra levels her wand at me, but I'm too angry to cower. These creatures are more like Mom than I imagined. Stealing someone's will and enslaving them to do their bidding . . . what is wrong with people?

Someone throws a tiny rock at my head. It grazes my eye and a small rivulet of blood trickles down my cheek. Thorn bellows and lifts up in front of me, taking a mighty inhale that can only mean a fireball is imminent—but whether he'll hurl it at me or the pixies is an open question.

Dominic

*B*eing at the Grove with Aurelia is surreal. She refuses to enter our houses and stands in the center of the field with her arms crossed over her stomach. A small group of police arrived with her, including Sheldon and Bartholomew the German shepherd—the Edge PD's official tracking dog. Alistair, Caspian, Iphi's sisters and her friends round out the group. Aurelia has brought one of Iphigenia's sweaters and Sheldon is holding it up to the dog's nose. Rhys and I hand out flashlights, whistles and bottles of water to the civilians.

Above us, Jared hovers in his griffon form. A long-time friend of Iphigenia's, he was the first to shift when Sheldon gave permission for civilians to join the search.

Sheldon ends his conversation with his deputies and turns to the crowd. "No one goes out there alone, you understand me?"

Everyone murmurs their assent.

"There needs to be at least two of you together at all times, preferably more, and we'll each take a direction. Bartholomew will follow Iphigenia's scent but clues could be anywhere, so we will spread out. For now, we have divided the Grove and its surrounding area into a grid, and after we divvy everyone up into search parties, Deputy Marquez will assign you a section of the grid. Do not stray from your assigned area or you risk missing clues. Everyone have a cell phone?"

We hold them up.

"Good. Don't use your cell as flashlights and drain your batteries. Use the ones Dominic handed out and keep your lines open. Call in to the station if you see anything. They will notify me directly."

"What if we need help immediately?" asks Iphi's sister Sadie.

"You blow your whistle."

Yeah, like that's going to save someone. Luckily, all of the people here are either Signum, cops or both.

Sheldon points a finger at Aurelia. "Aurelia and Alistair, you go with Rhys, Caspian and Dominic in group one."

Really? Not only will they hold us back with their slow walking, but Aurelia hates us. Well, she still likes me okay, but she hates my brothers.

"Burgundy, Elijah and Tiyah, you go with Deputy Marquez in group two." He points and the group shuffles together.

"Sadie, Ryder, Chrys and Carter— Wait." He turns toward those of us who work for the station. "A police officer or someone who works for the department must go with each group. Capisce?"

"Sure thing, boss. Should Cas and I split up?"

He turns to Rhys. "Caspian with Sadie's group, please."

I nod and move away with Aurelia.

Deputy Marquez walks around with maps to each group, assigning them to their respective grid spaces.

Aurelia puts her hand on my arm, leaning into my ear. "I'm glad you're with us. You're the only one of Iphigenia's suitors I trust." She narrows her eyes at Rhys's back, then growls, "Did you know your cousin is a cat?"

"Yes, ma'am, I did. He wanted only to protect your daughter."

"*I* protect my daughter." She thumps her chest with a fist.

Well, you're not doing a great job at it right now I want to say but don't. "Do you have any idea where she could be?"

"I will find her." Aurelia takes off, moving to the front of our small party, Rhys following close behind.

We walk for ten minutes, staying within our grid.

I know we need the search party so we don't miss anything. Jumping to conclusions is the quickest way to mess up an investigation. And yet, I know Iphi. I just *know* she's gone to the tree with the portal, and since I'm the assigned leader of this group, I steer the party in that direction even though it's outside our assigned area.

When we arrive at the tree, Bartholomew is barking and digging at its base. I could have saved them all of this, but perhaps a part of me was holding out hope I'd be wrong.

"The trail ends here," says Sheldon, leashing the dog. He looks at each of us in turn. Rhys is shaking his head. Alistair purses his lips and Aurelia has her hands planted on her hips.

I see no need to beat around the bush. "I fear she's in Brae."

Aurelia faints. Alistair catches her on the way down.

CHAPTER ELEVEN

THORN

There's something familiar about the flaxen-haired beauty, something that tickles right behind my scaled forehead. I hover in front of her face, gathering my strength to protect my mistress from her, when I feel it. An overwhelming sense of love, peace and acceptance. I blink and tilt my head. Faint waves of color emanate from her body and I let out a snort. She's trying to cast a spell on me?

Tossing my crimson-spiked head, I open my mouth to send out a stream of fire in her direction but she doesn't run. She stands there with blood running down her face, closes her eyes and holds her hands out to her sides, palms facing me.

"I love you, Thorn." The words hit me like a sledgehammer to the side of my skull, sending me physically somersaulting backward. I hit the ground and leap up onto my back legs, barreling toward her.

Iphi, my Iphi. My Iphigenia.

Without taking a second to wonder why I didn't know her only moments before, I tackle her. She lets me, but instead of hurting her, I nuzzle my face against hers. She giggles and tries to push me away.

"Thorn, you remember."

I lick the side of her soft face with my long forked tongue and she throws her arms around my neck.

Nolan the rat squeaks, reminding me that we aren't alone, and I leap off Iphi, blocking her from the still-angry pixies. I can only imagine my cousin has chosen to stay in his shift here because of the way they react to humans, but it's not safe for him with Astra, the animal controller around.

"I can hear you." Astra buzzes over us. "What else was I supposed to do when a terrifying *dragon* dropped out of the sky right on top of us? I didn't want to get eaten!"

Basil joins her in front of me. "It was purely for self-preservation."

Not if you can read my mind it wasn't.

"Can you blame me for wanting a watch-dragon? A protector?" She shrugs.

I'm not a pet. I toss my head and growl.

"What is wrong with you?" Iphi growls at Astra, the sound so enraged it knocks my own growl silent.

I've never seen her angry before—it's actually quite terrifying. I jump back a step.

"How dare you take advantage of Thorn like that? Take his memory? Make him do your bidding? What were you trying to do, make him your puppet?" Iphi's hands are on her hips, her hair waving in a nonexistent breeze, her jaw set and her eyes a flashing, jeweled blue.

She's not wrong and my scales ruffle at her words. Why would anyone try and control me? I'm a dragon! I'm the one in control! Maybe these little fairy creatures *should* fear me. I take flight and circle low around the brigade, debating whether to incinerate them all.

"Thorn." Iphi waves her arms above her head like an airline traffic controller. "Come down please."

Oh now she's trying to tell me what to do? Screw this. Fuck all y'all. I turn away from her and hover above the crowd, out of reach.

"Can we discuss this calmly please?" Bagaata zooms back and forth above my snout.

Nolan chitters to Astra from Iphi's shoulder. The pixie flies closer and Iphi tries to swat her. Not good.

"Don't escalate this." Bagaata flies between them.

"The rat wants to tell me something," Astra says.

Iphi glares at her. "Oh right, because he's your slave too?"

"He's not." Astra's lips tip down and then she pushes them out. "He says he's your friend Nolan."

Iphi sucks in a breath and turns to look at the rat on her shoulder. "Is this true?"

Nolan nods his head and Iphi grabs him and kisses his face repeatedly.

I dive toward them.

"Thorn," Bagaata snaps and I stop, hovering over Iphi. "Get this girl's temper under control or I will be forced to do it for you."

As if. *She's angry. I've known her for some time and I've never seen her angry before, only levelheaded and kind. She's also my brother's mate.* No point in trying to explain to Bagaata which brother, or how many . . .

"If she can behave, we'll give her a chance, but if not . . ." Bagaata clicks her tongue once, the tiny sound as clear as death.

Caspian

*T*he next several days stretch behind us like a never-ending nightmare. We take turns at Aurelia's house, Sadie's house, Chrys's house and the station. Each witch pores over their grimoire. Aurelia almost turns all of us into toads when she discovers the spell for entering Brae has been torn out of her spell book.

She tries her crystal ball, and we watch the past unfold as Iphi opens the door and gets sucked into the other world. We can even hear the Latin words she speaks but she's managed to hide the pages while she does it and no one can make out or guess the symbols she used.

Aurelia tries and fails. Chrysothemis tries and fails. Sadie tries and fails even though she assured me she'd juiced up her powers beforehand with a boisterous orgy. Ah to be a fly on that undulating wall.

Sheldon interrogates the ghouls. They refuse to cooperate. The only positive to come out of all of this is that Aurelia sees how much we care and how much we're willing to do for her daughter. She doesn't speak to us kindly—it's not in her nature— but her behavior softens, like cooking meals for each of us and offering us tea. It's not perfect, but it's a start.

Late one night, we're sitting on Sadie's front porch, drinking wine.

"Can we use a crystal ball to see into Brae?" I take a sip of the zinfandel. "Is there a way to see what's happening there, right now?"

Sadie and Chrys exchange looks.

"If that was possible, wouldn't Mother have said so?" asks Chrys.

"She's been overly distraught," says Sadie. "More so than I've ever seen her, so maybe not. I'll go get mine." She disappears into the house and returns holding her crystal. She sets it in her lap and then leans toward Ryder, her fiancé, who gives her a kiss. He moves a hand to her chest, fondling a breast through her cotton blouse. She cups his head, leaning hers back. His tongue darts out to lick down her neck while his hand plays with her nipple, now peaked beneath her shirt. He replaces his hand with his mouth, cupping her breast and teething the nub through the thin fabric. When she straightens her head, she's watching me through heavy lids, her mouth stretched into a wide smile. I look away.

Sadie is a sesso, a sex witch, so while the heavy PDA is to be expected, I'm just not prepared for it. Everyone else ignores them, or pretends to—it's rather difficult when they're front and center. Rhys and I exchange looks. I'm sure Dominic would too if he were with us, but since Aurelia likes him best, poor Dom's been assigned to mama witch duty. He's even sleeping in Iphi's room when he's not at the station. Poor guy. But we all appreciate the way he's taking one for the pack.

Ryder keeps giving as long as Sadie is taking, but finally she pulls back, her cheeks flushed with color. She sees me staring and winks. "Just be grateful I no longer have to reach a full-blown orgasm to get my magical juices flowing."

Oh my! My cheeks redden along with hers, though only mine are out of embarrassment. She flashes me a toothy grin and then focuses back on the ball resting in her lap. She passes a hand over it, closes her eyes and moves her lips in a silent incantation. My cousin and I watch the orb but nothing happens. After a minute she exchanges a look with her sister. "You still have yours in your car, don't you?"

"Yeah, I used it earlier." Chrys purses her lips and stands, walking out to the street.

"Why can't she just use yours?" I ask.

"They're not interchangeable. Unless spelled, no one else can even touch another witch's ball." She grins at Ryder. "I made one exception."

When Chrys returns with a velvet bag, I get up and offer her the seat next to her sister.

"Thank you." She sits and removes the crystal, holding it with one hand and passing her other hand over it.

At first nothing happens, but instead of stopping or becoming frustrated, Chrys's lips move and she leans closer to the ball, her brow furrowed. Still nothing. Carter stands, moves behind her and rests a hand between her shoulder blades. She visibly relaxes back into his hand and her brow softens but she doesn't stop her silent chant.

Quite suddenly the clear glass thickens with fog swirling inside the orb. When it finally dissipates, instead of Iphigenia's pretty face filling the sphere, a brown-tinged wasteland spreads out before us, swirling with a layer of ash. We all gasp as the globe pans along the horizon. Nothing at all appears to be alive.

Chrys exhales and looks up at Sadie. "I can't even believe it worked."

Sadie flashes her sister a tight-lipped smile. "I can. You're a seer and you're more powerful than you give yourself credit for."

"But where's Iphigenia?" Chrys echoes my thoughts, looking back down.

"She's there somewhere." I move closer to Chrys and study the ball. "Everyone here knows our girl's a fighter." Besides, if anything happened to her, I have no doubt that Dom, Rhys and I would feel it, physically. We're more than just emotionally bonded to our seraphim.

"He's right," Sadie says. "She may be innocent and sweet but that girl is straight-up warrior princess."

Chrys's eyes are misty when she looks back up and nods. "If anything happened to her, we'd know. Right?"

Sadie reaches out and touches her sister's shoulder. "No question."

I jut my chin forward. "Now we just have to find a way to bring her back." To us.

CHAPTER TWELVE

IPHIGENIA

I may not be the angry type, but I can't just stand by while anyone steals the will of someone I love. Thorn did what he could to calm me down, eventually herding me away from the others while Nolan spoke to them on my behalf.

They agreed not to harm me but they won't let me live among them . . . yet. I'm sequestered to a small, makeshift hut that Thorn slapped together close to the Nexus. It kind of protects me from the harsh elements but it has no sides, which means I basically live amidst the ash. The sky peeks through the haze now and again so the overhead cover is better than nothing and I don't want to seem ungrateful. The light in Brae has increased since I've been here—and it's not just me that thinks so. The pixies have noticed it too, but no one seems to know exactly why.

After a day of hiding in my shelter, Thorn appears, darting inside and landing on a small pile of ash. He cocks his head and blinks those red-rimmed, slitted eyes at me. A shuffling sound behind him draws my attention and I leap to my feet as a hooded figure approaches, seemingly dragging a lame leg. He's the size of a full-grown human and if Thorn weren't standing here, letting the thing enter my lean-to, I'd be terrified.

The creature speaks and there's something familiar, almost soothing, about his chapped voice. "Iphigenia, please don't be afraid."

I take a step closer and Thorn moves to the side. The creature enters my domicile and slips the hood off his head. I gasp. It's Taylor, my father.

"Dad?" I reach out a hand but dare not touch him in case he's a mirage. My rational mind is screaming. My emotions somersault in a tornado of confusion. I thought he was dead. He might be dying, given how terrible he looks.

"Iphi, my dearest daughter, I'm so sorry." He crouches to sit on the ground. "Can we talk?"

It takes every ounce of self-restraint to keep from throwing my arms around his fragile frame and never letting go. "It's really you? But—how?" I sit down opposite from him and Thorn turns to leave. "Thorn, stay, please." The mini dragon turns back and sits next to me. Whatever Dad has to say, I need a witness and Thorn is the one person—um, dragon —I trust the most here, in this desolate world.

Dad disappeared when I was six, and Mom told me and my sisters he was dead. Then two years ago, he returned—a slave at the Scrim's side. But he did everything he could to protect us, including betraying his master. I haven't seen or heard anything from him since he saved Sadie's life by returning to Brae with the Scrim.

"It's me. There's a long story, sweetheart, but I'm going to try and hit the most important points."

I nod but it feels like my head is on someone else's body.

"All of this started a very long time ago, before you were born," he begins. "I had recently moved to the Edge. I was hired by the Council as a psychologist to vet the humans who wanted to move there as part of the human resettlement project. They didn't want a bunch of people that were crazy about living near Signum, or crazy enough to want to kill them."

I never knew this. If Dad and Mom spoke of why he moved here, I was too young to remember. A heaviness settles in my stomach but I say nothing, only nodding again to encourage him to keep going.

"I'd lived there for less than a year when, one moonlit night, I was walking down the beach alone —this was before I met your mother, you must understand. A wave rose in front of me and then froze. Having lived among Signum for a few months, I wasn't afraid but I should have been. I didn't know any better and so I stood there, waiting. A spiral appeared at the center, whirling this way and that, and suddenly I couldn't move at all. It was as though I was glued to the ground and hypnotized. When the portal opened and the face of the Scrim appeared, I was terrified—"

Dad stops, shuddering. I don't have to imagine the fear he must have experienced at such a sight. I've seen it myself, after all. I can't hold back anymore. I reach out a tentative hand and touch his knee, some part of me expecting him to disappear at the contact. Inch by inch, Dad's hand reaches for mine. He's real. His fingers are rough with the ash engrained in his thin, papery skin, the nails jagged and torn to the quick. These aren't the soft, kind hands of the strong man from my childhood, but it's him nonetheless. Dad takes a deep breath, his grip firming as if resolving to finish what he's started.

"There was nothing I could do. He possessed me,

it's the only way I can describe it. I was aware of the things I did after that initial hypnosis session but I couldn't stop them."

"What things?" My voice is small and shaky. Thorn puts one talon on my knee and I place my free hand on top of it, the coarse scales comforting me.

"He wanted your mother."

"My mother! Why?" I leap to my feet.

Dad follows, holding his hands out flat. "That's her story to tell, but please, hear me out. Then if you never want to see me again, I'll respect your wishes."

What in the Goddess's name could he have to tell me that would make me never want to see him again? After losing him—twice—and finally getting him back, all I want is to hug him close and never let go. "Whatever you have to tell me, I'm here. Please, continue."

"The short of it, and the important part, is that I . . . sought out and pursued your mother. Most of the time the Scrim's influence didn't affect me. The only way I can describe it is that I was like some sort of sleeper agent. My mission was to get close to Aurelia and lure her back here, to Brae. But all I *felt* was the need to get close to her. And when I did, I fell in love with her and fell hard."

My heart races with the revelation, but I force

slow breaths to calm it. He was enslaved by the Scrim. I knew that, of course, but I had no idea it started so long before I was even born. Their whole marriage was a lie? Some scheme by the Scrim to achieve . . . what? But was it a lie? I do remember them being happy. Truly happy. That couldn't have been an act. "Go on," I take a seat again, crossing my legs, and he follows, slowly, as though he's aged a thousand years.

"Life was good, for a long time. She got pregnant with Chrysothemis, then Sadie and of course, you." Outside, the sunlight seems to grow a fraction brighter, limning his features. His smile is so bright when he looks at me, his gray eyes crinkling in the corners where permanent crow's feet have set in.

Does he know that Sadie was the result of my mother's affair with a sesso? That she's not his biological daughter? No, now is not the time to bring that up.

"But the Scrim came back for his due. He found a way to make human anchors on Earth, since he couldn't set foot there on his own. With his power divided between me and the anchors, my mind began to clear. Or maybe my love for you all helped me cut through the fog, I don't know. All I know is one day, I woke up and knew you were all in danger.

He had plans for you. Deadly ones. My children. I couldn't let that happen. So I killed the anchors and fled. I ran as fast and as far from the Edge as I could, away from you. I knew he would be too preoccupied hunting me to do anything to you. It was all I could think of to help you. I exchanged my freedom for your lives but he eventually caught up and . . ." He spreads his arms wide. "Here I am, a former shell of myself and the Scrim's dog."

Tears sting my eyes and I blink rapidly to hold them at bay. He killed someone. Multiple someones. The thought is revolting and tragic and how do I deal with knowing he did it to save me? My own father gave his life, his freedom, to save ours. Without thought, I tackle him with a hug so fierce it not only tumbles Thorn from my shoulder, it knocks Dad down too.

"My Iphigenia." He strokes my hair.

*S*everal days later, Thorn takes on my usual role as the diplomat and convinces the pixies to let my father and I move a little closer to the hive.

We move the lean-to, my father and Thorn helping. So much of our time, it seems, is spent trying to extend the miniscule food and water supply. Apparently nothing has grown here in years, but in the past week or so, tiny shoots have begun springing up over the landscape, though none of it is large enough to eat yet. Their ocean dried up long ago, which means it no longer teems with sea creatures, so that's not an option. The pixies require little sustenance and when their planet started to die, they began to hoard. Dad, Thorn and I are surviving on a trivial quantity of nuts and grains, growing feebler by the day. Even so, we're a massive drain on their resources and there's nothing we can do to stop it.

"I know of a place where there may be food," Dad tells me, "but it's too far to walk."

"Thorn can take us." I rub my hands together.

Dad shakes his head. "He's too weak. There used to be small animals hiding in the ash. I haven't seen any in over a year, but with the new plant growth . . ." He shrugs. "It's worth a try and there may be some edible vegetation growing again too." Without waiting for agreement, he bends to kiss me. "I'll be back as soon as I can."

I don't want him to leave, fearful he'll never return. I just got him back. All of these years without him and now we've been reunited. But he's doing what he needs to do, in the spirit of helping us, and I respect that. I stand mute as he gathers a staff and some sharp sticks, looking behind once and smiling at me before shuffling out into the clearing haze. It takes every muscle fiber, every cogent cell, not to run screaming after him, to hold myself in place. I crumple to the ground, staring after his retreating figure.

Thorn scuttles over and wraps his small wings around my shoulders, nuzzling my neck with his thorny snout. It tickles and I turn toward him with a wan smile, swallowing the lump in my throat.

"Hey, sweetie," I whisper. "You've been my rock here." Not just my physical protector but also my emotional anchor. "If we ever get out of this and you become a human again, I'm going to hug you for weeks and shower you with kisses."

His forked tongue darts out to lick my cheek and I wrap arms around him and let the beast comfort me with his presence.

When the light dims again, indicating it's night-time—the muted diurnal cycle another apparent change in Brae, according to Dad—Bagaata, Astra and Basil bring me herbs, gemstones and sacred objects. They've finally softened their stance on my efforts to cast some magic. I'm grateful because I need to focus on something right now, something less painful, something to pull me out of myself and help us find a solution to Brae's resource problems. I unsuccessfully try to conjure up food. When that doesn't work, I cast a circle and then another, finally able to expand Bagaata's protection spell over Nexus. With her help, the spells are even more powerful, and I'm fairly certain the Scrim can't come near their center.

While waiting for Dad's return, I also try and fail to change Thorn back to his human form. Selfishly I want my big, strong, muscled man in his human form. I want to wrap my arms and legs and climb him like my silks. I want to do what I said I would and press kisses to his face, his lips, his broad chest. If I'm completely honest with myself, I want him to take me. I spend more than a few moments fantasizing what that would be like. Sex with Thorn. I have to fan myself over the imagery. I don't imagine he'd be sugary sweet like gentle Caspian. Nor would he be overwhelm my every sense like intense Rhys. He most certainly wouldn't focus on my every reaction like attentive Dominic. No, sex with Thorn would be raw and wild. Sex with Thorn would hold me in the present moment and keep me there.

Sex with Thorn—now where the heck are these thoughts coming from and why can't I force them out of my mind? No matter, as long as that's where they stay. I allow myself another few minutes trying on the fantasy before I berate myself that most women don't have three lovers, let alone four. But why should I feel guilty for needing more than other women? My men are happy with the arrangement. What would they say if I proposed adding Thorn to our stable?

CHAPTER THIRTEEN

THORN

I watch Iphigenia when she's performing her spells. I watch her when she eats the pathetic amount of food we can scrounge. I watch over her while she sleeps. She's a small slip of a woman with so much untapped power, so much misunderstood potential. Every day I'm with her, every minute, every second I fall a little harder. When I was under Astra's mind control, the only thing that pulled me out was Iphigenia's sweet, sweet voice telling me she loved me. What's left of my human brain knows exactly what she meant but my animal brain wants to believe she meant that she was *in love* with me because fuck, I'm pretty sure I'm damn close to being in love with her.

A rat approaches, chittering up at me. Food! I

open my maw to devour it when Iphi shrieks, "Thorn, stop, that's Nolan!"

The rat scurries over to her and she bends to pick him up, placing him in *my* spot, on her shoulder. Red stains my vision and I consider plucking the thing off her shoulder with my teeth. I can almost hear the bones crunching in my mouth. The rat hisses at me, unafraid. I do a double take.

Oh shit, it *is* Nolan.

Wet guilt douses the hot anger, and realization slams into my thick dragon skull. I almost ate my cousin.

Maybe having him stay in his rat form wasn't the best idea after all. Sure, he can walk freely among the pixies and they listen to him like he's some ancient being, but if I lose my marbles and accidentally eat him, I'll never forgive myself. Killing someone in order to protect my pack is deplorable but killing *one of my pack* is unforgiveable.

"It's okay," Iphi coos, first to Nolan and then to me. That woman is a real-life saint. "I know you didn't mean it. You're not in your right mind."

Understatement of the year.

Nolan squeaks in her ear and she pets him, sitting cross-legged in the ash because without enough food, walking far takes up too much energy.

I join her and she lets me put my head in her lap.

There is *nothing* sexy about this place or this situation, and yet . . . I close my eyes and let myself imagine what it would be like if I were one of them. The fourth in Iphi's pack.

When I wake up, she's spread out and asleep too. With a dwindling water supply, we've had to conserve even more energy. The ever-resourceful pixies found a way to tap below the desolate surface and are harvesting enough liquid for the town. For themselves. It's barely enough for me, Iphi and Taylor, since we need so much more than they do, but at least it's more than we had.

Iphi's father has been gone for two nights, wandering alone on the playa without food or water. But he's been living here under these harsh conditions for over a decade. Still, I know she worries, even if she doesn't express it out loud. Her fingernails are bitten down to the nubs, a habit she acquired the day he left.

We're curled up together, resting at the base of the pixie stronghold, when I first catch a whiff of Taylor and jump up.

"Thorn, what is it?" Her words lack vitality.

Scanning the horizon, I spot him and push my pointed muzzle against her arm, nudging her upright. I point with a wing and she squints and then leaps to her feet, scrambling toward his silhouette. I follow her but the man moves faster than we do, even with the staff across his shoulders. I smell meat too before I see it hanging off the staff. Small animal carcasses for me, not for Iphigenia. She no longer eats meat but I've no doubt he's found edible roots and nuts for her. He's done it. He's saved us.

Several hours later we've eaten less than we wanted to, but I've done enough survivalist training to know you shouldn't gorge your body or it can go into shock. Taylor also helps the pixies tap deeper into the underground well, using his strength and knowledge of Brae to bring up enough water for the big people.

Showing up with food not only endeared Taylor to the pixies, who were leery of him before, but also to Iphi, who's dropped every ounce of anger and pretense toward the man.

For the next day they're practically inseparable and while I'm happy for her, I deeply miss our time together.

"My father has an idea," she says the next night at dinner. "We've already gained a lot of strength back and he wonders if you can fly yet."

Not hesitating to show off to my woman, I lift into the air, slightly surprised that I am indeed able to soar. Iphi smiles up at me, the pink hue of her lips an unconscious invitation, her recently pale face suffused with happiness.

Bagaata flies alongside me. "I'm happy to see you well again." Her voice is clipped but she doesn't hide the tenderness in her eyes.

Iphi waves for me to land and I do, nuzzling up to the side of her leg. Bagaata hovers in front of us.

Iphi crouches down to stroke my back and wings, addressing both of us. "Dad knows of a place, somewhere he thinks my magic will work. He's too weak to go himself. He still needs to recover after his hunting trip. But if he gives you directions, can you take me there?"

Twenty minutes later, Taylor has repeated his directions to both of us. For the fifth time. I may be a dragon, but I'm not an idiot. And my tracking skills are without equal. Somewhere deep within my lizard brain, there's still a tiny kernel of reason that reminds me if I kill Iphigenia's father, I won't get the girl, so I dutifully stand by while Taylor quizzes me, with Astra's help, and Iphi goes off to pack some supplies.

Bagaata flits around, making sure Iphi has all of the herbs, crystals and other magical items she may need gathered into a small sack. Taylor fills another one for us with some food and water held in an animal skin.

"Pei used to be our main source for fresh water," says Bagaata, "so you may be able to find some there but if not, if you run out, come back, even if the spell is not complete. Understood?"

Ready to depart, Iphi nods and then hugs her father. Then I hold still while she ties her two bags to my flanks.

In less time than it would take to stalk a sunbathing lizard, Iphi dangles from my talons as I follow Taylor's directions toward some type of citadel carved from a natural rock formation.

After what seems like a very long time, we approach a darkened city, its blackness looming at least a hundred feet high. My heart thumps in my chest. I don't know where we are, I've never seen this place, but I do know it's not protected from the Scrim since no one's cast a spell over it. It looks like someone took wet mud and dripped it from their hands to form a structure—a giant mud castle with a great jutting spire. The closer I fly the more reflective the surface becomes, jutting skyward like glass shards. Blackness reaching into blackness. I circle the shorter towers. The place is as silent as a grave. Here's hoping it won't become ours.

At Iphi's suggestion, I fly us to the uppermost tower and set her down on a terrace. Iphi falls to her knees, her little hands petting the reflective surface.

Obsidian. I land next to her, my red scales glinting in the black reflection of our new landscape.

"This entire city is made of obsidian?"

I nod, blowing a puff of fire from the side of my mouth. It does nothing to the volcanic glass. Dragon-proof, nice.

Iphi unhooks the food bag from my flank and sets it aside. The other bag has cinched tight around my middle during the flight, and she scrabbles at it with her fingernails. It takes most of my patience to sit quietly while she loosens it, and when she finally gets it unattached, I heave a sigh of relief. The herbs and magical items she packed spill out and onto the hard floor.

She drops down to scoop everything back inside, then freezes, staring at her reflection beside mine, clear and bright in the surface below.

"Thorn, look. The reflection—it's so clear. There's no haze or ash here."

Huh. She's right. We're standing on the tallest terrace of one of the many cathedrals, and from here, we can see practically miles in every direction, though the horizon is the muddy haze I've come to expect in this forsaken place. Bagaata explained that no one built the cathedrals, but it's difficult to fathom the land creating something that looks man-made.

Iphi cries out. I whip my head back to her, but her face is alight with joy. "That's not the only thing that's cleared up here. This place—I'm me again. I'm back! And, Thorn, I know exactly what I need to do."

I have no idea what she's talking about, but anything that makes her smile like that can't be a bad thing.

I sit back and watch Iphigenia standing on the black terrace, raised to her full height, her arms stretched overhead. She looks taller and more foreboding than I've ever seen her. She looks bolder, wilder. An untamed version of herself, so similar to that of her mother I have to blink several times in order *not* to see Aurelia. Her blond hair lifts up in that breeze that only seems to appear when Iphi is angry. There's even a red hue suffusing the air around her that I never noticed before. Her flaxen curls whip about her flushed face, the gusts escalating.

"Hail, guardians of the watchtowers of this land. I call to the past spirits of Brae, the ancestors of old, Pei the volcano that formed this city."

A gust of wind shoots by, one tangible even to me now.

"I call in the wind to wash away the old, to wash away the past and usher in the new."

She's daunting in her newfound power. She's

calling in the freaking *wind*? Witches can do that? And it's a monster wind, one that blows the soot, ash and silt away. A wind that ushers in the smell of growth and renewal. In this moment, she is one hundred percent her mother's daughter. Only my unmitigated trust and love for her allows me to stay rooted to my spot instead of running and cowering in the lee of the tower behind us.

Her hands glow red with a light akin to fire but it's not fire. It's magic, and her whole body vibrates with it. She holds one hand over the bag of her supplies, and out rush herbs, implements and stones. They circle in front of her, first slowly and then faster until their speed is so they've become a blur—one that is whirling right toward me.

I open my mouth to roar and the items fly into my gaping maw and down my throat. Coughing and sputtering, I collapse onto the ground. Above me, the fire witch brings her hands together and a red ball of energy erupts between her fingertips. The ball glows brighter and stronger, turning her blue eyes red with its light. Her flaxen hair is now bloodred.

Is it too late to snatch her up in my maw and fly her away from here? Bringing her here was a mistake, one that may cost me my life, though that doesn't scare me. What does scare me is that it may cost Iphi hers.

Before I can lift off, she throws the huge ball of fire directly at me, and it slams into my body like a bowling ball, flattening me. I lose my breath, my sight, my mind. As everything I've ever known slips away, I try to reach out for something to anchor my being, but soon all is oblivion.

CHAPTER FOURTEEN

IPHIGENIA

ower courses through me like a thousand dragons, as though all the fire and all the light from all the dragons in the world are mine for the taking. It's nothing I've ever experienced before. The sensation is beyond my imagination, beyond my wildest dreams. It exceeds thought and common sense, blotting out the Iphigenia I was and ushering in a rebirth. The Iphigenia I'm supposed to be.

How dare the Scrim devastate this land. How dare the pixies enslave Thorn. And why is everything left up to me to fix? I'm the one who has to defend the Edge. I'm the one who has to give the ghouls their lives back. I'm the one in Brae trying to save Thorn and Nolan. No one else is doing anything. The ineffectual council and police force sit with their thumbs up their bums. The only ones trying to help are Cas, Rhys and Dom, but they can only do so much, and why should they be the only ones on the front line of this war? Why should they risk their lovely skins for a whole town who'd never return the favor? Fuck this shit! I should just grab Thorn and Nolan, go back to the Edge and let the pixies deal with their own drama. Then I'll show the Edge what I'm *really* capable of. They want me to fix everything for them? No problem. I'm strong enough and powerful enough to take over and show them *exactly* what their petty squabbling and short-sightedness will get them.

The expression on my dragon's face is pure fear and rapture. His eyes are wide, forced open from the heat radiating from my body. From my hands. His mouth hangs agape, his throat moving to swallow the myriad of tiny herbs and substances that fly down it, but I feel removed, as if I'm watching two strangers from above with no care for the outcome.

Even though his fear is palpable, I can't comfort him. I can't stop the power that's coursing through me anymore than I could stop the sun from shining over the Earth.

I turn my back to him. His heart is breaking but I don't care. I can't. If I stop for even a moment, none of this will work. I've tried for days to access my magic, but surrounded by dead things that held no energy, no light, I was blocked. But here, everything is different. Here we are surrounded by the product of something that was once alive—and still is. Below us, the mass of a powerful volcano still holds within it the light of creation. Now it's my light, mine to shape and force to my whim.

The sounds of tearing flesh and bones fill the dead air around us. I focus on the magic, holding it steady as the monster becomes man once again.

When the tearing and crunching stops and the moaning begins, I turn around and crouch to gather the man in my arms. With just a little more focus, I can use my newly amassed power to punch a portal open above us and rise like a phoenix from the ashes, Thorn clutched in my arms. I can even pull Nolan and Dad up with my power once we're through and then I'll lock it behind me so these creatures are imprisoned in their hell forever.

"Iphigenia." Thorn looks up at me, his eyes unfocused. "Have you gone mad?"

Before I can respond he kisses me, and the shock of it, the tenderness and force of it, slam me back into my body. The only thing filling my consciousness is him. My anger, my plans for revenge, my psychopathy—all gone, replaced with his insistent lips, his soft breath, his drugging moans. If his mouth weren't so all-consuming, I'd be shivering over the hypocrisy and insanity of it all.

Instead, I melt into him as he kisses the last shreds of my inhumanity away and then I'm able to return the kiss with fervor. Our bodies wrap around each other, caught in the lover's embrace we started just a few months ago. It seems like decades, eons even, have passed since we last kissed, at Promise, on the dance floor with the heavy thud of trance overhead.

This time it's so much more. This time I'm ready. I give myself to him, letting him explore my mouth with his tongue, my lips with his lips. I sigh into him, all thoughts of the Scrim and Brae and ghouls obliterated. Instead, I'm with him. His presence. His vibrancy. His domination. Melting in his embrace, I let myself be held by this strong man, so drained and sleepy from the use of all that power. Power that saved Thorn and then unraveled my very soul. He pulls me in tighter, moving his mouth from mine to my cheeks, my forehead and the top of my head. My eyes grow heavy as my dragon kisses me to sleep.

Dominic

. . .

"*D*ominic, dear, it's time for dinner," Aurelia calls through the closed door of Iphigenia's room.

The woman never enters without knocking first. And even that is rare. Mostly she calls my name from outside the door. I have to admit that she's growing on me no matter how much I try to resist her charms. She's steadily becoming the mother I never had, the one I always dreamed of.

How did I tame the wild beast that is Aurelia? I'm the only person she won't lash out at. She's even losing it at Alistair instead of at me.

"Be right there, Mama." She insists I call her that. I close my laptop. No more research. It's not yielding a thing and it's driving me batty. I've seen enough patients to realize that Aurelia is projecting on me, but what can I do about it? I can't call her attention to it, so all I can do is call it what it is in my own mind and do my best not to piss her off.

When I get to the dining room, she's set an impeccable table once again.

"You don't have to use the silver and china every night I'm here."

"It makes her happy." Alistair takes his seat at the

head of the table and reaches for my glass to pour me some sparkling water.

"Plus this is a night for serious discussion." Aurelia passes me a plate of Instagram-perfect lasagna and I spoon some onto my plate.

"Serious discussion?"

She waits until we all have food and then looks at me. "I can help you find Iphigenia, but you will need to shift and go get her."

"You can find her? In Brae?" I pop a bite of lasagna into my mouth, chewing slowly. I'd rather not eat after that bomb she's dropped, but if I don't, she'll take it as a personal affront. Aurelia is an old-fashioned woman—literally, she's 186—and still takes offense when someone doesn't enjoy her food. No matter what else is going on.

She finishes her own bite and reaches for her glass of prosecco, sipping it slowly. As she takes her time, I sit on my hands and count to ten, keeping a pleasant look on my face. I could write an entire textbook about this woman. She's a walking case study, wielding almost every emotionally manipulative tactic I've spent my professional life studying. And if the psych books in the hallway bookcase are any indication of Iphigenia's father, he must have needed them to keep up with her as well.

Right now she's withholding. It's a power move

used by people who don't feel like they're able to maintain their power at all: say the first part of something important and then withhold the rest. The only way to get Aurelia to finish what she was saying is to pretend like I don't care. I cover my mouth and fake a yawn, take a sip of my water and look at Alistair, opening my mouth as though I'm about to change the subject.

"I have installed a tracking device on my youngest daughter. I tried to use it to bring her back here already but it didn't work. If you can get into Brae, I can give you a talisman to lead you to her."

This time my professional demeanor deserts me. I drop my fork, lasagna sauce flying. Aurelia frowns at the spot I've made on her pristine tablecloth, but even so, I can't help but grin. Yes! This is exactly what we need.

Alistair, nonplussed, looks at her with raised brows. Apparently this is the first time he's heard about Aurelia's habit of lojacking her children.

"Thank you, Mama! You're amazing. How long will it take you to make it?"

Aurelia smiles despite herself, preening. "Not long. I had to special order new belladonna since mine was spoiled, but it should arrive here tomorrow."

"Wonderful. Then you can open the portal and

my pack and I will go get her." I pick up my fork, appetite renewed with the good news.

But Aurelia goes still. "Yes, well . . . About that. Despite my best efforts, I can't seem to open a portal. Or rather, I can open one on Earth, but I can't make it connect to Brae. I can't see or sense her on the other side, so there's nothing for my magic to anchor itself to."

Anchor. There's that word again—it seems Aurelia's magic and the Scrim's work along the same principles. I slump in my chair, rubbing a hand down my face, trying to think.

Wait, Aurelia couldn't *see* Iphi.

I sit up again. "Have you tried looking for her through your crystal ball?" There's no way I'm about to tell her that her sisters have already tried and failed, of course, but even they acknowledge how much more powerful she is.

"Of course, dear. It's the first thing I tried the last time—" She goes quiet, then shakes her head and smiles at me. It doesn't reach her bicolored eyes. "It didn't work."

"The last time?" Alistair asks.

She waves a hand at him. "I misspoke."

Bullshit. This woman never misspeaks. She's hiding something. But no matter how practiced she is at hiding, I'm better at uncovering. I lean back in my chair and cross my arms over my chest, keeping a blank look on my face. After a full minute, I look at my plate and commence eating but I'm watching her from my periphery.

Her eyes dart left and then right. She smooths down the front of her dress, purses her lips and sucks in a breath of air.

Yup, she's lying about something, and I'm going to find out what it is.

CHAPTER FIFTEEN

IPHIGENIA

I wake in Thorn's embrace, unsure of how long we were out. My head rests in the crook of his arm and when I move my eyes up to his face, he's awake too, looking down at me. I offer him a bright smile, acutely aware of the proximity of his hard body, all angled ridges and swoon-worthy muscles. I sigh aloud and nuzzle into him. Rough hands glide up my back, pressing and kneading my sore muscles,

"Thorn," I whisper and then breathe in his scent. Sweat mixed with earth, our Earth, back home. He smells like home and a tiny groan escapes as I nuzzle his firm, corded chest. The flesh between my legs aches and throbs. Is he about to make my fantasies come true? I freaking hope so.

His large hands slide over my waist and hips,

clutching me there and holding me captive. His darkened eyes roam over my face and I heat under his heady gaze.

"I want you." My voice squeaks instead of coming out husky the way I'd intended but it doesn't seem to matter.

His mouth plummets down on mine, sucking at my lips and forcing his tongue inside. I press back, my hands exploring the hard planes of his muscled back.

Pulling me down on top of him, I tangle my legs around his, my tongue with his. I arch my breasts into his chest. One hand circles my waist, grasping me there and then moving down to cradle and squeeze my ass. There is no way to ignore his hard cock growing full beneath me, and I grind against it.

"Oh God, Iphigenia," he growls. "I want you. I've always wanted you." He tugs at my breasts, squeezing so hard I almost shriek but the plea-sure/pain of it shrinks the sound in my closed throat. He flips, pulling my body astride his like it weighs nothing. Moving one hand away from my ass, he fists my hair, tugging my mouth down to his, his breath hot and fast. The ground must be so hard underneath him but he doesn't seem to notice. His hand dances over my chest, squeezing and twisting my nipples through my shirt. The sensations wash over me.

His mouth is warm, his lips hard and his tongue like molten lava. It presses into me greedily, taking what belongs to him, laying claim.

"Get naked. Now," he rumbles, letting his dragon out or not yet able to rein it in.

I stand to strip. His tongue swipes his full lips as he watches me, and he puts his hands behind his head to prop himself up. "Slowly. So I can enjoy the moment I've waited an eternity for."

I'm no burlesque star like Burgundy, but I keep my eyes on him while dragging my fingers up my torso to the collar of my long-sleeved cotton shirt. I undo the buttons one at a time, stopping to caress each exposed patch of skin, before letting the garment fall from my shoulders. Then I turn and bend over to shimmy out of my jeans, giving my hips an extra sway all for him.

He watches, unblinking. His breathing deepens, catching in his chest, the sound loud in the absolute quiet of this dead world. The walls around us echo our moves. Hands reach up to clutch mine and though I'm naked and vulnerable, the way he looks at me, the cold hellscape around us disappears. I place my hands into his and he stands, the motion lithe as he uses his powerful abs to rise without putting any weight on me. Our fingers intertwine as we stand face to face. Well, more like face to chest. This man is tall, the tallest of his brothers and the thickest from all his years of hard play. Where Rhys is lean sinew, Thorn is chiseled granite. He looms over me, the stark contrast between us intoxicating. He keeps ahold of my hands and steps back.

"Delicious." His voice is deep and gravelly. His gaze travels over me, sparking heat from the center of my belly all the way out to my fingertips and toes. "You are the most beautiful woman I've ever seen."

"What are you gonna do about it?" I tease.

"You're gonna fucking find out." He wraps his arms around my naked body and scoops me up. Breathing into my neck, he licks up the length of it, nipping just to the edge of painful at the tender skin.

Our bodies press together so tightly there's not a molecule of air between us. Trickles of sweat bead on our skin, melding us together.

"Oh Iphi." He cradles my head, twining his fingers in my hair, tugging my face up for a kiss. His passion and fury are exactly what I imagined from him and I love it. He's fulfilling a desire I've had my entire life, a deep need to be consumed by lust. The way Caspian, Dominic and Rhys make love to me has no place in this den. Thorn is raw and wild, untamed. The bad boy every woman wishes to experience at least once.

His kiss is demanding and hot, filling my mouth, filling my senses, blotting out earlier sweet ones with a desire all its own. His groans fill me and his rigid, thick length throbs against my stomach. I shift and reach down to reposition it and he bites my tongue. Not hard, just enough to send tingles up my spine and back down my arms. He pulls back to nip my lips, his pulsing cock pushing into the muscles of my belly.

His hands beneath my ass and my legs wrapped around his waist, he walks forward to Goddess knows where—and then I'm shoved up against a wall. "Stand here for a minute," he orders and puts me down. I do as I'm told and lean back against the cold, hard wall, which quenches the heat pouring off my skin.

Thorn kneels in front of me and I grab the top of his head, his hair a velvety, honey-colored fuzz because he hasn't shaved it in weeks. He sits up on his knees to press kisses along my collarbone, his hands skimming down the sides of my body, past my breasts and then stopping at my waist. His mouth descends on a nipple, taking it into his mouth and flicking it with his tongue, then clamping down to saw it between his teeth. I groan and lean my head back with a thunk against wall. He bites down on the nipple and I cry out. He loosens his teeth and moves between licking, sucking and biting, softer this time. One hand cups the tender skin of my breast, now alight with shooting nerves. The other hand moves lower, over the plane of my stomach to cup my mound. Fingers press against my opening and he switches breasts, taking the other nipple forcefully.

I expect him to speak again but he doesn't. His finger teases my opening, swimming through my wetness and spreading it up around my clit. I bite back a moan and my legs shake. Keeping one hand on a breast, he rubs the palm of his other hand against my hard nipple and works down with his mouth, kissing my ribcage and stomach. His fingers work at my clit, pinching and rubbing it. Twirling the nub between his large fingers. When his mouth hovers over the sparse hair above my folds he moves his other hand down to my pussy and drives a finger through my moisture into my tight cunt.

My legs weaken and I lean against the wall for support. He buries his face in my mound, breathing in and out to the point of distraction. It tickles and yet the sensation is exquisite, his warm breath feeding my nerves, exciting my clit.

Suddenly, the hand that was touching me there wraps around my butt and squeezes, his fingers digging in hard. I whimper, though at least now he's shouldering some of my weight. It's just as well, given how much my legs are shaking, but I still want to complain—until he buries his mouth where his hand was. The jolt of ecstasy almost brings me to my knees but of course Thorn would never drop me. His massive body will never let me fall.

His tongue is warm and huge, covering my entire clit and half my pussy. I expect light, tight licks but he grazes his teeth over my sensitive skin and I whine with pleasure. His mouth clamps onto my bud, hard and hot, sucking and pulling me into the scorching heat of his mouth. The nerves explode, zinging and zapping like my own personal fireworks display and I groan in pleasure as waves of sensation trip up and down my legs. A finger still works my opening and when he plunges two inside, I lose my balance completely, falling forward, draping my torso over his head. He stops and both hands clench my inner thighs, hard, shooting me upright.

"You will remain standing and come in my mouth," he growls.

I sputter, looking down at his hard features. This is Thorn in his element, taking complete and utter charge. *God yes.* I prop myself against the wall and spread my palms to either side of me, feeling along the black glass for a handhold and not finding one.

Thorn returns to his task, opening my legs wider first, which helps tremendously. A wider base I can hold—until he attaches his mouth between my legs once again and my knees weaken. It's a game. I have to switch focus from his talented tongue and mouth to my balance, which makes the game last longer. Much, much longer.

The dragon man alternates between licking and sucking, at first widening his tongue and lapping at my clit and lips. Then he wraps his wide mouth around the entire area and sucks while fingering me into oblivion.

As I force my butt to stay upright against the cold stone, my orgasm builds. But instead of starting between my legs in my pussy as it always has, this one starts low in my belly, like a flame that grows with each lick and devours with every suck. My mind empties. I forget about the wall, forget about standing, forget about my other men. The only thing in this moment is Thorn and me. The sparks of sensation grow into a blaze as my orgasm tears through me, spreading like wildfire, erupting like the jet of lava that formed this obsidian cathedral at my back. Pure white sensation explodes from my belly, forcing out everything else. It travels up my spine and shoots out of my arms. It travels down my pelvis and shoots out of my legs. My whole being vibrates with bliss as the sensations crest and then ebb.

It's not until the last molecule of pleasure has drained from my cells that I realize Thorn is standing in front of me, holding me up. His hands are under my armpits, his mouth is on mine. His cock is a rock, standing straight up and pushing against my stomach.

Thorn

*I*phigenia is a goddess and I could die a happy man after watching her come for me. But I'm also a greedy man. And I want more. I want to make this woman come over and over and over. I want to make her scream my name until she cries out for me to stop so she can catch her breath before I ravage her all over again. Dragon and man war inside me. The man doesn't want her to feel obligated to fuck me just because I got her off. But the dragon is ready to beg.

She reaches down between our bodies, but the thought of her delicate hand on my painfully hard cock is almost enough to let the dragon take over. I push my torso into her so her hand gets trapped before it can touch me. And I keep kissing her. I take my time with her mouth, rolling my tongue against hers and then pulling it out to lick her lips and kiss them hard. She brings my beast out. I can play soft and nice but by the way she bucks into me and bites at my lips, she's not averse to a little rough. Her free hand reaches around and rakes my back with her fingernails.

"I need you to fuck me," she growls into my mouth. "I need you to bury your cock inside me. I want all of it. I want all of you."

I have to grab the wall behind her to keep from crashing to the ground at her words. My mind is reeling. Looks like dragon and man can stop fighting at last, united in pleasing this angel.

I grab each globe of her perfectly toned ass and lift her up. She wraps her legs around me just like before. I hold her high and slam her back against the smooth wall. She looks down, between her pert breasts, at my cock.

"It's so big," she gasps, licking her lips. Her brows are creased as she looks back at me.

"You can change your mind. This is about you."

"No, I need you. I need to feel your length. I need you to fill me up."

I growl deep and loud, leaning forward to take her plump lips, sawing them between my teeth before sucking them, pulling them in. One hand still on her delectable rear, I reach between our bodies, grab my cock and rub it against her swollen pussy. She gasps in my mouth and I push my tongue in, sampling her sweetness.

I keep my cock hovering right below her entrance, teasing her, swirling the head in her wetness and giving her time to adjust, but she's not having it. Her legs flex as she drops her body down and my cock slips into her slick canal. It sucks me up to the hilt and she groans, breaking the kiss to lean her head back.

Her pussy clamps around my dick, sending lightning through my body. Electricity shoots from my organ, lighting a path straight to my heart. It's the exact instant where erotic pleasure and love merge. I had no doubt that I loved this woman, but in this moment, I can acknowledge that I'm deeply, crazily, tail over snout *in* love with her. And I will do anything to keep her. Happily share her with my brothers. Happily share her with my cousin. Happily take a back seat even. As long as she'll have me.

"Iphigenia." My voice is thick and deep.

"Thorn," she murmurs against me.

"You're mine," I snarl.

Her head falls forward and her eyes snap open as she holds my gaze. "I'm yours." Her perfectly shaped mouth curves up and mine does the same. She leans forward, kissing me, bouncing on my cock again. Her pussy and thighs clamp around me, putting paid to the lie of my words. She's not mine—*I'm hers.*

It almost pushes me over the edge but I want to wait for her. She comes first. In my life, in our bed, in everything. This woman has captured me heart and soul and I can't help wanting to merge with her completely.

Breaking the kiss, I manage to croak out, "Come with me."

"I'm close," she breathes and her pussy clamps around me again.

Oh fuck. I bite the inside of my cheek and enjoy the ride, helping her fuck me by rocking her back and forth, up and down, side to side.

She grinds down on me, rubbing her clit hard against my pelvic bone. Her breath hitches and her pussy tightens even more. When her body stiffens I know she's a few seconds away from exploding and I ease up on the inside of my cheek, ignoring the bitter tang of blood.

Her body spasms and I let myself go. With her eyes open, never once looking away from me, she wails and pumps, tightening her legs around me and pushing out with her core. I hold her bottom as she arcs away from the wall, her head falling backward while her tits reach for the sky as only a contortionist could. The movement pushes me deeper inside of her and her contractions pull my orgasm to the surface, where it was locked and ready.

Those same electrical waves shoot through my dick and then back up my body, climbing up my spine. With nothing tethering me to reality, I soar over the brink too, skyrocketing down into the unknown depths below. I follow it without holding on to it, just riding it, freefalling into the space she's created for me. For us.

CHAPTER SIXTEEN

CASPIAN

$\mathcal{D}$ominic and I are talking to Deputy Marquez about the ghouls in the holding cell when Sheldon walks in.

"Can I see you two in my office for a minute?" he asks.

Dom and I exchange a look and he pats Marquez on her shoulder. "We'll finish this later."

We follow the chief toward the front of the station, where he holds his office door open for us. It's utilitarian like most things cop and he motions for us to sit on the receiving side of his battered metal desk while he files in to sit behind it.

Placing his elbows on the surface, he leans forward, his bushy eyebrows lifting. "I was hoping I could convince you two to take the graduate exams and become actual officers of the law."

This is out of nowhere. "Why?" I ask. "We both love what we do, and we're helping the force already. Do we really need to be 'official'?"

"You do if you want to carry firearms and help protect our city. I'm not asking you to leave your current jobs; we need you two here in the capacities you already serve."

"But?" Dominic leans toward him.

"But with all the ghouls and the history of the Edge being a target . . . You know about the things that have happened in the past?"

"Trackers?" I ask.

"That, and unsavory witches, rogue vampires . . ." He steeples his fingers and taps them together. "Even if the ghoul threat ends sometime soon, quite frankly, it'd be nice to have a few more people I trust carrying weapons if it's needed. You could legally carry and use handcuffs, carry a police radio, and help your brother."

So that's it. But he can't know Thorn's in Brae. We've been covering for him. "Help him or replace him?"

"Help him, of course. Plus, we could use more shifters on the force." He leans back in his chair. "You don't have to make a decision right this second, but I know you've both done some preliminary training with Thorn. It'd just be a matter of taking a couple exams to certify that you've assimilated what he taught you, maybe taking in another class or two to fill any holes Thorn left. I can deputize you while you do that and get you on the street in the meantime. Easy peasy."

"We'll do it," says Dominic.

I twist in my chair. "What the hell, Dom?"

"Look, Cas, I have my psych degree and you have your masters. I love my job, but there are plenty of times when my skills aren't needed and even more times that you're not required to come in and sketch a person of interest. This will give us more flexibility. We'll be able to work more, help Thorn and the Edge. Plus it'll let at least one, if not two of us, stay home with Iphigenia," he swallows at her name, "if she needs us."

Because she *will* be back. Anything else is unacceptable.

I cross my hands over my chest and set my jaw. "Fine, but I still want to be your go-to sketch artist."

"Always," says Sheldon. "I'm glad you both agree. I already set the exams up for you in the conference room."

"What, now?" asks Dom.

"Don't back out on me now," I tease.

Sheldon grins. "Come now, you two could pass these with your eyes closed. Let's do this."

"What about the ghouls?" I ask.

"What about them?" Sheldon stands up.

"Deputy Marquez says that only a few more have been brought in." I stand and Dom follows.

"I don't think any new ghouls are being made at this point," Sheldon says as he leads us out of his office and down to the conference room.

If there are no more ghouls being made, then maybe the Scrim no longer has an anchor here. That would be great news if true.

When we enter I'm not surprised to see a stack of papers set up at opposite ends of the long table. There's already an officer sitting and waiting for us.

We both sit in front of our respective piles of paper. Sheldon nods once and turns to leave. "Thank you both. I'll be happy to welcome you to the force. Officially."

The paper on the top tells me to wait until the officer says we can begin. Great. Tests.

Thorn

"*C*an we talk?"

She sits up, faces me and hugs her knees to her chest. "Of course."

Yet it takes me a minute to find the words I'm reaching for. Not a surprise, since I haven't had to use any in a while. I rub my face, surprised to find a full beard has sprung up while we slept. It must be what happens when a male is stuck in a shift for such a long time.

"I'm sorry if I've been unsympathetic," she says into the silence. "You must be going through a lot right now. You've been an animal for so long . . ."

"Yes." I incline my head. "That's part of it I'm sure. But the crux is that I lost control."

"It's to be expected." She reaches a hand out and I give her mine. "Your dragon took over."

"That's not really how it felt, though. What if," I look up at the sky and then back to her soft eyes, "my humanity was taken from me?"

"Taken? How?"

"I've spent long stretches in my shift before. Not that long, but long enough to know what happened to me wasn't right. The spell your mother cast—I'm not saying she erased my humanity on purpose but what if that was a byproduct?"

She squeezes my hand. "I've never heard of

anything like that but . . . she did turn Sadie into a mouse once. My poor sister couldn't stop eating cheese for a week." She lets go of my hand and shifts to sit next to me. "I'm so sorry my mother did this to you. It's unforgiveable."

"No Iphi, it's not."

"Why do you say that?" She places her hand on my knee.

"Because she's your mother and she had her reasons. It was wrong but I don't want you to hold on to that grudge. Besides, if what she did was unforgivable, how can you ever forgive me?" I look down at her hand. I want to touch it, hold it, but will she regret the contact once I've come clean?

"You haven't done anything wrong, Thorn. You can't blame yourself for your actions in your dragon form. No one was permanently hurt."

"But that's just it, Iphi, someone was. You were so shocked and hurt when Taylor admitted what he did to get away from the Scrim. At least he had no choice, but me . . . Years ago," I swallow my inner coward and turn my head to look into her eyes, "I accidentally killed a man." A flash of Ted screaming and spinning on fire floods my mind, along with the ever-present remorse and pain I usually stuff down out of my conscious thoughts.

I expect her to shoot up and run but she doesn't.

She holds my gaze and reaches for my hand with both of hers. I could swear something touches my forehead too, but the sensation passes before I can even be sure it's there. "It was a complete accident." Her voice is slow and soft. "You were so young, and you were only trying to protect your pack."

Wait, what? I leap to my feet. "How do you know that? Are you inside my head?"

"It's my gift." Her voice is so quiet I can barely hear her.

"What the hell kind of gift is mind reading? Without permission?" I turn away from her. The sense of exposure, of helplessness is back. I just shed it in her arms—my human arms, the ones I haven't had in weeks—but after only moments of freedom, my mind is once again subject to the whims of another. That it's Iphi invading makes it worse, not better.

"I'm sorry, you're right. I can't always control it." She rests a hand on my back and I war with myself, wanting to shrug it off and walk away, and wanting to turn around and hold her.

"Iphi, I've lost my free will. Don't you understand that? Your mother stole it from me, then Astra and now you too?" I spin around to face her but the look on her face melts my fireproof heart. The way her eyes are so open and earnest, the way her hair falls around her face in a mass of loose curls, bedhead at its best. The way her tiny pink rosebud of a mouth is unhinged, just a fraction, like she's searching for the perfect words to cut through all of my pain.

"I've been so blind, so insensitive to your needs. What can I do?" Her hand trips down the flesh of my arm, sparking goose bumps.

"Oh, Iphi." My heart soars at her touch, with love, not lust—but that's there too, potent and surging. She wants to understand, to make it better, and she acknowledges my pain. There's nothing greater.

I lean toward her and kiss the top of her head. She throws herself into my arms and I wrap her up tight.

CHAPTER SEVENTEEN

DOMINIC

*N*ow that Caspian and I are officially official, I have to tread lightly. Though I can't complain—it's been good to be fully included in the ghoul investigation. We've helped round up a few more. Thankfully, without another anchor, they haven't become an epidemic. We'd have nowhere to keep them locked up if they did. Though it sucks that all we can do for now is contain them until Iphi gets back.

But she *will* be back.

Spending more time at Aurelia's instead of my house is wearing on me but I remind myself I'm doing it for Iphigenia. Caspian, Rhys and I haven't been able to find a way into Brae. No one's seen Nolan or, thankfully, the Scrim. He's probably too busy with our girl. The thought leaves my skin itchy, as though a thousand ants are crawling over it. It's up to me to find out what's going on. I'm the one who can.

Another night in Iphi's bed without her and I lie awake for hours, waiting to make sure that Aurelia is sound asleep before assuming my small shift. It's the one I keep hidden from everyone except my brothers.

Once I'm tiny, I sneak out of Iphi's room on my eight legs, scurrying up a wall on the other side of the door. If Armageddon sees me, he will chew me up and swallow me in two seconds. Actually, he'd probably bat me around and play with me first until I'm almost dead. Then he'd eat me.

A cat is a spider's worst enemy.

But even if I *were* poisonous, I would never hurt anything or anyone that Iphigenia loves.

And almost as if the cat knows I'm trying to sneak out, his black paw tries to flatten me as I scurry under the doorway. Could he smell me? Hear me? Or is he Aurelia's familiar and able to sense when someone is plotting against her?

He presses down on my spindly frame, but I slip between the pads of his paw to freedom. Once on the other side of the door, I scurry up the rough wood grain. Not deterred, the cat leaps into the air and slaps the door with his paw. Right next to my head. Shit, he'd better not wake Aurelia.

I crawl along the ceiling where the killer cat can't reach me and drop down in front of Aurelia's door. The killer cat thwaps me with his paw, sending me flying like a golf ball through the small opening underneath the door. Safe. Or as relatively safe as one can be while breaking into the bedroom of the most powerful witch in the world.

I climb through her dresser first, in case her journals are hidden among her clothes, but I just end up covered in silk and lace. She may have them hidden in her closet but I chance the elaborate rolltop desk next to her bed first, climbing beneath the closed cover. Here I'm rewarded.

I worm my way inside the book, crawling between the sheets. It takes the better part of another hour to force the book open and scan several entries. Good thing it's paperbound and not leather, the spine worn and the sheets rice-paper thin.

The woman is hiding so much from so many, but the full story is not between these pages. Still, there's enough here to learn that she lost her firstborn children over a hundred years ago in a place that sounds suspiciously like Brae. And there are several mentions of someone named Auberon. Best of all, there's what look like the rudiments of a portal spell.

I need this book and there's only one way to get it. For that, I have to risk all of the time I spent building up Aurelia's trust, but it can't be helped. *You're doing it for Iphi*, I remind myself and so this is just another setback, for her. If Aurelia loves her daughter as much as I know she does, she'll forgive me.

I crawl from between the pages and scurry back to Iphi's room, keeping to the ceiling as much as I can so the spider-killing cat doesn't pounce. He certainly earned his name with me. Once inside I shift back, dress and make sure the front door is ajar for my impending escape. Then I creep back to Aurelia and Alistair's room, feeling pretty damn skeevy. There's not much point in trying to sneak in without waking the woman—I know that's not possible—so the element of surprise is all I've got here.

I rub my hands down the legs of my jeans and put my hand on the doorknob. Okay, I can do this. I turn the knob, dart in, throw open the desk lid and grab the book.

"That's mine," screeches Aurelia, moving like lightning out of her bed.

"What's going on?" comes Alistair's sleepy voice.

"I'm about to turn this ungrateful boy into a mouse," she hisses.

I book with the book as fast as I can out of their room, down the hallway and out the front door. As I'm fiddling with the key fob to my car, unlocking the door with a bleep, I chance a look back. Bad idea. The woman stands in the doorway, hair flying, eyes blazing, and she's pointing an actual wand at me. Better for distance casting? I have only a second to react as she jerks it up and then down. I hold her book in front of me like a shield with one hand and open the car door from behind with my other. The force of her spell knocks me into my car and I quickly touch my arms to make sure I'm still human. Yep, all fingers and toes accounted for. I dive into the car and press the start button on my Prius while she's gearing up for another spell, her mouth moving and the wand still pointed at me. Tossing the book on the passenger seat, I peel out of her driveway and this time, I don't look back.

Thorn

While Iphigenia sleeps, I explore the ancient city. My angel will probably be thirsty when she wakes. Maybe I'll get lucky and find a forgotten well or pool or something. The walls are high, like a fortress, but still the pale green sky stretches above. Green, a color no one here has seen in the sky for a century, according to Taylor. It now shines with the bright intensity of the green pools in Antarctica, in the Amundsen Sea, where I once went ice climbing. The pixies often refer to the emerald green sky of Brae, the violet sea, the lush plants and flowers so vibrant it hurts to stare at them for too long. We're not there yet, but it is obvious this planet is awakening.

I wander through corridors carved from lava flows. No one mentioned a volcano here, but there must be one. Active? If so, I can always shift back and carry Iphi away. I'm not worried about losing her now; I can sense her presence like a lighthouse flashing at a wavelength just beyond what my eyes can see. Can anyone else sense it too?

Something slithers over my bare foot and I jump, looking down, but nothing's there. I enter a cavernous room with seats carved into the walls. Above the seats, a series of strange symbols adorn the rest of the space and I move closer to study them.

A small gust of air winds past and I get the distinct feeling that I'm being watched.

"Hello?"

There's no response besides the echo of my words reverberating against the cold walls of the chamber.

Maybe if I sit and offer no resistance, whoever is hiding will appear.

While I do so, I contemplate my pack. My circumstances. The woman I have now claimed as mine too. How will they react? Will they be open to dialogue? Either this will bring our pack closer or it will rip us apart. We *will* be sharing in a common goal. We won't have to posture or fight over who gets the girl. We won't have to be in competition with one another. It's a triple, no a *quadruple* win situation. But I may be the only one who sees it that way.

We each offer her something unique. Rhys can introduce her to the rest of the world, enticing her beyond the Edge's walls. After all, he was the one to pull her out of her shell first. He can guide her toward protecting herself, inside as well as out.

Caspian can share his vision, his artist's eyes showing her things the rest of us miss. The breathtaking photos he'll take of her and share with the rest of us will be a heck of a bonus.

Dominic, her touchstone. He will ground her and help her decipher her thoughts and emotions, keeping the bright cacophony of the world from overwhelming her sensitivity.

And me. Not only can I be her partner in adventure, I can protect her from the sometimes harsh realities of life, soften the blows that come her way. Not that she needs it—the woman is scary strong. But she won't have to face the hard times alone, not anymore.

For us she brings it all together in one complete and perfect package. A woman who can't be contained or owned. A woman who can't belong to just one man.

There's another tickle on my feet and this time it doesn't move. Then there's a titter and a rat runs up my bare leg to perch on my thigh.

"Nolan? What the fuck?"

He points a paw back toward the opening of the cave and chitters loudly.

"May I remind you that I do not speak rat? Why did you follow us here? You're supposed to be in Nexus."

He leaps off my leg and runs toward the doorway, turning to look back at me with his beady black eyes. And that's when I hear it, a cackle and a shriek that can only be one thing. The Scrim.

Caspian

*R*hys sits at the kitchen bar in my house while I putter around in the kitchen. The morning sunlight flashes through my round, leaded windows. Neither of us have heard from Dominic this morning, which is odd since he usually checks in first thing and it's almost eight already.

"We should never have agreed to leave him alone at that witch's house." Rhys scrubs his face. None of us have bothered to shave in days, and though we haven't approached mountain man status, we're getting there.

I cover up my agreement by pouring my cousin a glass of fizzy water to go along with his coffee.

Rhys grumbles a thank-you and takes a sip.

Dominic bursts through the front door without knocking and we both practically spill our coffees, Rhys leaping up from the counter and me slamming my cup down.

"We've been worried sick and you stopped to take a shower?" Rhys narrows his eyes at Dom.

He closes the door behind him and holds up a book. "While I was running for my life in the predawn morning, naked, I didn't have a lot of options." He slams the book down on the countertop and I approach it cautiously as though it's a snake about to strike.

Flipping open the cover, I'm greeted with meticulous writing. The dark cream of the paper looks handmade and the looped sienna strokes are achingly beautiful in their elegance, written with a fine-tipped fountain pen.

I shake my head and fetch Dom a cup of coffee.

"What is it?" Rhys reaches for the book and flips to another page.

There are drawings scrawled in the margins, so fine in their detail I pause from my task to hand my brother a half-poured cup.

"This," Dominic takes a sip and taps the book with a pointed finger, "is one of Aurelia's many journals."

We both look up at him with wide eyes.

"And she knows you stole it?" I'm shaking so hard I have to clutch the counter to stop.

He nods. "She does and she may come after me

but she wants her daughter back just as much as we want her back."

"What the hell, Dom?" I slam my fist on the counter. "You've purposely pissed off the craziest, most powerful and most vindictive witch in the Edge? On purpose?"

"Hear me out." Dom flips a few pages and taps the book again. "Iphi is in Brae."

"We already know this without having the fucking book," I snarl.

"Caspian, chill for a minute and look." Rhys's voice is a lot mellower than mine and I want to wring both their necks. But I peer over his shoulder instead.

There's a drawing of something flying, a fairy maybe, with the name *Auberon* scribbled above it. A red X covers the drawing, the lines so forceful they've gouged the page. The text around it is a hodgepodge of English and something that's probably Greek or Latin or Italian, but certain words stand out anyway. *Carina*, *Speranza* and *Igina*. And then the word *Brae*. Some symbols line the other margin, indecipherable but clearly witchy.

"What is all of this?" I ask.

Dominic lets out a fatherly sigh. "From what I can decipher, and my Latin is rudimentary at best, this creature, Auberon, killed Aurelia's three children over a hundred years ago."

"What children?" Rhys asks.

"Another family she had before, I think." Dom takes the book back, flips toward the end and shoves it back in my hands, pointing to an elaborate symbol on the page. A familiar symbol. Underneath it are the words *Iphigenia* and *Chrysothemis*, but the latter is crossed out with one black line through it.

"That's . . . that's . . ." I'm too dumbfounded to speak.

"The brand on the back of Iphi's neck." His jaw tightens. "Apparently it's Aurelia's version of a GPS. We can locate our girl using this."

"But we know where she is. She's in Brae. How the hell will this help us? We can't even get to that world." I want to add the word *asshole* but clamp my mouth shut just in time.

"One thing at a time." Dominic is annoyingly calm. "We can't go into Brae blind. I've seen it in Chrys's magic ball; it's not a tiny land and we don't want to be wandering around looking for her without food or water. Or worse, fighting off hostiles. We need to find out where she is first. Then we go in and get her."

"Do tell, Brother. How are we supposed to get

inside this world?" I don't bother keeping the sarcasm out of my voice.

Dominic flips several pages back and taps a page. "See here?" There's a drawing of a vampire foaming at the mouth, a spiral floating behind it. "If we can get ahold of a ghoul, we can get into Brae ourselves."

"And how do we get a ghoul?" My doubt is starting to give way.

"That's where we'll need her sisters and someone to distract Sheldon while we break a ghoul out of holding." Dom takes a sip of his coffee as though breaking into the station's holding cells is something we do on a daily basis.

"Uh, that's illegal, dude. And we're the law. Officially now. We could lose our jobs for that."

"Which is why I'll do it." Rhys slams his glass down and stands.

"And risk getting caught and maybe prosecuted?" I slam my own glass down. "Now that's a good man."

"Taking one for the team." Dom claps him on the back. "Thanks, Cuz."

It does make the most sense, but since Rhys is often the odd man out among the four of us, I would never have suggested it and I know Dom wouldn't have either. "So what do we need for this plan to work?"

"Gather some supplies. Our new police gun belts,

loaded guns, extra ammo. Walkie-talkies and the rest of our arsenal. First aid kit, water and food, flashlights, knives and a rope. Whatever else you can think of, as long as it's light." Dom swigs the last of his coffee and turns toward the front door. "Meet me at the police station in two hours."

"Where you going, Bro?"

"To figure out how to get Aurelia to cooperate."

"Yeah, good luck with that," Rhys says.

I shudder. "Don't get turned into a toad, dude."

"I'll have to take that chance. Hopefully this is where my psychology degree will pay off." He winks at us and walks out the door.

"I guess this is where you and I gather the supplies?" I take my backpack and gun belt out of the closet and Rhys runs back to his house for some things. While he's gone I throw in a few plastic bottles of water, then run over to Thorn's and dig out a couple of his LifeStraws and fire starters. The guy's closet has more camping gear and sports equipment than clothing. We may not need any of these items, especially if we shift, but Boy Scout motto and all. I was never a boy scout, of course, but I always wished I were.

An hour later we're waiting outside the station for Iphi's sisters and our brother when I get a text from Dom. *This is going to take a little more time. Can you two pull off getting a ghoul and then meet me at the tree?*

Sure thing, buddy. I'm not feeling as confident as I sound but no need to stress him out. I'm happy we're finally doing something to save our girl. Sitting around for days with our thumbs up our asses was not working for me. I'm sure I've either developed permanent high blood pressure or I was on my way to a heart attack.

I show the phone to Rhys and he nods, chewing on the inside of his cheek. The guy looks like he hasn't slept in days. We all handle stress differently, that's for sure.

A few minutes later Sadie and Chrys pull up with their significant others. The girls get out of their car and into ours.

"Ready?" Sadie asks.

"Not really," Rhys and I respond simultaneously.

"Great, this is definitely going to work then," mumbles Chrys.

CHAPTER EIGHTEEN

THORN

"*W*here's the girl?" the Scrim snarls from outside the doorway.

Nolan runs back and hides behind my legs. I square my shoulders, set my jaw, raise my chin and march out of the room. Overhead, looking down at me, is the white moon face of the giant, all gaping maw and teeth. He's tripled in size at least and reaches a hand down to snatch me by an arm, yanking me skyward.

Dangling in the air, my legs scrabble for purchase. He leans his face close to mine. "I said, where's the girl?" His breath is putrid and I gag, swallowing repeatedly. A forest of shark teeth glistens in the green light.

"What girl?"

"Scrim," Nolan shouts from below. He's transformed back into his human form and I want to scream at him to hide. Goddammit, I can handle this. "Let him go. It's me you want."

The Scrim laughs, the sound like the ominous screech of a climbing axe sliding down into a crevasse.

"I'll take you to the girl," Nolan shrieks. "Just let Thorn go."

Da fuck? I pin him with my gaze, as small and insignificant as an ant. He glances over at me, an eye twitching. His tell. He's bluffing.

The Scrim drops me and I flail all the way down, careening off an embankment of hard rock where I tuck into a ball, the way Rhys showed me. Gotta practice falling if you're gonna learn to fight, he always said. Great advice. Mental note—thank Rhys, if I ever see him again.

Nolan's mouth opens but no scream escapes as the Scrim stoops to pick him up. But when his hand is about a foot away, it freezes, then he clutches and grasps at the air just in front of my cousin's body. Right—Iphi's amulet! But a moment later, something beyond the edge of hearing or sight snaps, and the Scrim's enormous hand wraps around my cousin's body with a grunt. He picks Nolan up in my stead. Nope, the amulet is obviously Earth-bound magic only. Shit. I use the distraction Nolan's providing to shift into my dragon. My large dragon. The massive beast that does not fuck around.

The pain of the shift is excruciating and I bite back a wail to maintain the element of surprise. The Scrim is busy walking with Nolan around the other side of the cathedral where Iphigenia is not. Thank you, Cousin. Just please hold on.

As soon as they're out of sight, I take flight, working hard to keep the flapping of my wings to a minimum. By the time I've coasted around the cathedral, the Scrim has figured out that Nolan has played him and he tosses my cousin high in the air. I swoop up to catch him, losing my advantage in order save his life. It's not a difficult choice but it's one I wish I didn't have to make. Nolan flies through the air like a surfboard tossed over a giant wave. I thrust my bulk below him and catch him on my back.

"Ooof," he grunts, the wind sucked from his lungs on impact.

Meanwhile, the Scrim is stomping around the glass cathedral, attacking it with his massive hands. Splinters of glass fly through the air and I turn my side to them, raising a wing to protect Nolan. I'm peppered with shards that tear through my leather wings, the pain agonizing.

"Put me down and kill that thing," Nolan yells in

my ear.

I'm not deaf.

"Over here." Iphigenia's voice cuts like a blade through the surreal landscape.

I bank toward it. She's framed on a balcony atop the highest tower, arms raised high, hair whipping in the wind like a medusa's head of a thousand snakes. Her body is alight with flame, glowing a bright red-orange under the chartreuse sky. But she's not on fire, she *is* the fire. Flames shoot out from her hands, her hair, blazing from her entire being, so powerful I can almost feel it from where I am. I claw through the air, but as my heart races with adrenaline and time slows down, it's like I'm diving through molasses. I'm so far away. I race toward my beloved, but the world stretches in front of me. I'm so far—

Too far to save her.

The demon reaches down with his gigantic hand and plucks her glowing form from the tower as though she's a tiny blossom. She looks at me and nods her head once, then mouths, *Trust me.*

I expect him to scream in pain when his hand meets her flame but instead it dies out, snuffed, and like King Kong sweeping Fay Wray off the Empire State Building, he plops her on his palm and smiles at her, those rows of teeth reflecting all the pain and sorrow of this lost world.

I am almost to them, flapping my torn wings as hard and fast as I can, but with all the tiny tears my speed is cut in half. Then the monster turns his smile on me. He purses his lips and puffs out a stream of air that blows me off course. I whirl in the air, mantling my wings to stop my spinning and regain my path. But when I finally do, with Nolan's body wrapped around my spiked neck, they are both gone.

Dominic

*A*fter poring through Aurelia's book with my brothers and finding nothing other than a lot of personal information that she's obviously withheld from her family, we've run out of options.

Slinking back to the wicked witch's house and ringing her ominous gong sends a physical jolt through my system. Every single shred of common sense I possess is telling me to run, but I stand my ground because, at this point, we're out of options. I don't know what she will do to me and even though

I texted Alistair on his cell to make sure he'd be here too, I can't count on him to save me from Aurelia's rage.

And yet she answers the door with a civil nod, decked out in her housecoat with Alistair standing behind her like a statue of a butler.

"You have some nerve." She narrows her eyes at me and holds out her hand. "Give it back before you enter and I may let you live."

I place the small journal into her outstretched palm. "I apologize." I keep my voice steady and sincere, making eye contact with her single brown eye and avoiding the blue one.

She crinkles her nose and spins around, leaving the door open like a gash. Alistair nods once and steps aside, closing the door once I enter. We follow the wicked witch into the kitchen, where she places the journal down on a counter far from the table and motions for me to take a seat. I sit at the table and Alistair sits across from me, reaching out to take my hands across the table. Is that meant to be comforting?

Aurelia saunters past to stoke the fire lit in the hearth below her swinging cauldron. A metal staff is plunged into the flame, the handle resting against the large black metal pot.

My eyes widen and I look between Alistair and Aurelia. "What's going on?"

"You want to find Iphigenia, yes?" Alistair asks.

The witch twists the iron rod in the open fire.

"You know I do, but I thought . . ."

She spins around, glaring at me. "You thought what? That it would be easy? That you'd click your red heels together and spin around three times reciting *there's no place like Iphigenia's heart?*"

"You said you installed a tracking device on her. Can't we look on your phone to see where she is or in your crystal ball?"

Barking out an evil laugh, she puts her hands on her hips. "And that will help you how?"

"It'll give me an idea of where to start once I get into Brae."

"First of all, idiot," she turns back and spins the stick again, "you can't get into Brae without an escort."

I look at Alistair and he nods, still holding on to my wrists.

"You need to be with someone who lives there or someone who's connected to the world through one of its inhabitants. Otherwise, you can't cross over." She pulls the long metal spike out of the fire, twisting the staff in her hand.

"This," she inclines her head toward it, "is not

only your ticket into Brae, it will guide you to Iphigenia once you're there."

The glowing red symbol at the end wavers and dances in my vision. It's the same mark that's burned into the back of Iphigenia's neck.

I try to rise but Alistair easily holds me in place. If it weren't for his vampire strength, I'd be out the front door by now.

She approaches me with the burning emblem and I wiggle in my chair, trying to knock it over.

"No point in fussing." Her voice is sour. "Take it like a man. Iphigenia put her head down without a word. I expect you to do the same."

She's right, I've been bested. This was my wish, kind of, and it's too late to back out now. I do as she says, watching the brand disappear from my peripheral vision.

The temperature rises as she lowers it slowly toward my flesh and I fight with myself to keep from flailing.

"That's a good boy. This will only hurt for a very, very long time." Her voice brims with sadistic pleasure as the burning-hot metal meets my flesh.

Someone, somewhere is screaming in agony. It takes me several seconds to realize it's me. The room spins and the table rises up to meet my face.

CHAPTER NINETEEN

RHYS

*T*he scheme seems destined to failure from the start. I agreed to take one for the team and all, but I'm nervous for us. It's dangerous, there could be an accident, we could get caught . . .

I may be the right man for the job, having the least to lose, but hopefully when Sheldon finds out why we did it, he'll drop the charges. Either that or he'll make an example out of me. It's too late anyway; I'm all in. No use thinking about it now.

I spend several minutes tugging on my hair, chewing the inside of my cheek and rubbing my face with my hands. None of the nervous tics work. I practice the deep breathing Master Chin taught me back in New York and then the alternate nostril breathing I learned from my days at the ashram.

When everything fails, I sit with my back against

the cool stone of the building, close my eyes and wait. The girls are casting a spell from the back of my car and then, on cue, the fireworks begin. Of course, since fireworks are illegal in this drought-stricken state, it doesn't take more than about three minutes for most of the police force to bolt out of the station. By the time they arrive, Dominic has left to drop the girls back off with their boyfriends. Can't get caught red-handed.

I make my move and slip inside the back exit, using the keypad on the outside of the door. Luckily, the code Caspian gave me still works. No surprise, they don't change it that often.

Of course there's a guard stationed inside, but Sadie's cast a sleeping spell and he's out cold.

I slip the key card out of the guard's pocket and approach the cell where the ghouls are being held.

"Well, well, if it isn't our follow compatriot," one of the ghouls lisps.

I hold the card up. "I'm getting you out but I have a condition."

"You let us all go . . . and we won't kill you." The ghoul talking is tall, about six feet six, and he's more coherent than any of the others.

"Not a chance. I let you out and only you. You open the portal and I let you go free. Come back here on your own and release your friends if you so desire. I'll hand you the key card and tell you the code."

His laugh is hollow, yet full of mirth. "If you were still part of our renegade brigade, you wouldn't need me to find the master." He runs his long fingernails over the bars, creating that screeching sound that drives grown men crazy, me included. I look back at the guard; he's snoring but he won't be out for much longer. Shit.

I shrug nonchalantly, feeling anything but. "Yes or no?"

He doesn't reply.

"Your prison, not mine." I turn to leave.

"Take me," hisses another ghoul. "I can open it." Then, a rasping, choking sound.

I whirl back. The large ghoul has wrapped both hands around the other one's neck, dangling him off the ground. He looks at me. "I'll do it."

"Put him down." I narrow my eyes and the tall one drops the other, who crumples to the floor. "I'm going to open this cell but if you all rush out, you'll be stuck in this holding room with no escape since you don't know the code to the door. That means you and only you." I point to the large ghoul who's positioned himself in front of the others. None of them look too coherent anyway.

He nods. "Call me Leo. You have my word." Then

he laughs, a wet sound erupting from the back of his throat.

"The rest of you move back against the wall." I wait until they obey and then touch the key card to the pad. The gate slides open and the tall ghoul slides out. They're on a timed mechanism and less than ten seconds later it slams shut. As Dom explained, in order to hold it open for longer, the key card has to remain in front of the sensor.

Once outside the cell, the tall one moves toward the back door, trying to open it using his strength alone. It doesn't budge. When he turns back to me, I cock my head and raise my brows. He narrows his bloodshot eyes and lets go of the handle.

"If you do as I ask and lead me there . . ." I waggle the key card in front of him. I omit the fact that Dom'll be by in minutes to "suggest" to Sheldon that the department change all its codes and key cards ASAP, given the jailbreak.

He steps aside and I punch the code into the keypad, swinging the door open with a bang.

Iphigenia

*T*he Scrim spirits me away in his enormous hand to a strange black hut in the sky on the other side of the island of Brae. Either my amulet doesn't work in Brae or the beast means me no harm.

The hut is more a fortress at second glance, one that sits atop an enormous, craggy peak The building is made of broken shards of obsidian stacked together like a mortarless puzzle. When we arrive, he takes one giant step around the doorway, too big to enter the hut, and sets me down on a black balcony jutting out from the structure. The slab of obsidian that forms the lookout appears to be wedged directly into the mountain itself. Then the beast returns to his normal—though still large—size, shrinking down like a flower without water next to me on the overhang. He must have built his glass prison himself while in his gigantic form.

Cobbled together or not, it's still obsidian, and something about the material in this world means I yet again have full access to my ability. I reach a tendril inside his head.

Though I expect to find violence and anger within the giant's thoughts, there's only confusion and anxiety.

It's like he's at war with himself. I see quick

flashes of empathy for others, overpowered by waves of anger and destruction. As though a switch has been turned, I'm suddenly drawn into his head, like Alice falling down the rabbit hole into a swirling mass of chaos. On the other side is a bright white light and I find myself propelled out into space where I hover midair, face-to-face with a child fairy. I'm inside his head, glimpsing the past.

"I want to learn to hunt," the young boy says.

"And you will," the Scrim/I responds.

"How? When?" The little boy zooms back and forth in front of the Scrim/me like a hummingbird.

"I will teach you when the time comes," says the Scrim.

"Promise?" His already tinny voice rises an octave.

"I promise." The Scrim's voice is warm and melodic. I don't recognize it at all.

And the only emotion I sense within this memory is love. I sigh and then, in an instant the scene is gone, ripped to shreds to reveal a nightmare of destruction beneath. The Scrim, a giant demon, rages through the obsidian city, crushing tall cathedrals of glass while thousands of pixies cry out and scatter.

The strangest part of this memory is that there's no connection to the former one. The only emotion here is anger. In everyone else I've known, memories connect themselves like pearls on a string. One begets the next, united by a single subject or emotion or association. Even when someone is subsumed in thoughts and memories of rage, they still maintain a thread to their humanity.

But with him, it's as though that thread was snapped. As though he has no access to that which came before. I blink several times to disconnect and crouch down on the weathered obsidian, leaning my back against the side of the platform. "You hurt so many people to get me here. You have me now. What do you want from me?"

The Scrim takes a step forward, but having seen that somewhere, hidden deep inside, this monster is capable of love, I don't shrink back.

He collapses down on the stone in front of me, puts his elbows on his knees and sighs. He doesn't look like the big bad he is. He looks like a confused, lost puppy.

"Being near you brings back some of my memories."

Inclining my head, I wait for him to elaborate.

"This past century, I've felt nothing but rage and hate and the need to smash everything to pieces. I've beheld no memories save one."

He turns his head and looks down the mountain.

"And now?"

"And now I'm starting to remember bits and pieces." He barks out a hollow laugh. "I think the memories may be worse."

"Why?"

"Because now I'm beginning to remember all that I've lost. All that I've hurt. All that I've destroyed." His voice catches, like a hiccup.

"But why did you do it?" His loss and longing is palpable.

"Because I was cursed. Turned into this monster. That memory is forever burned into my skull." He turns toward me and then quickly looks away, blinking.

This big, bad demon is so lost, so utterly misunderstood. Cursed. What could have changed him into something so opposite his true nature? "Who did this to you?" And why?

He ignores my question, flashing his shark choppers at the jade-colored sky. "I wasn't always a monster."

I nod and push a curl out of my face.

He looks at me and shakes his head. "I was loved by all. But that was so long ago. Another lifetime."

"What happened to you?" I ask softly, not wanting to break the spell lest the raging psychopath return.

He looks right at me, holding my gaze, with those unblinking, blackened eyes. "Your mother happened to me."

"What?" I screech. I jump to my feet, putting one hand on the rock wall to steady myself.

"She's the one who did this to me." He doesn't sound angry, just confused, like he's sifting through distant history that happened to someone else.

How the hell can he sound so remote about this? My mind reels, so much so that I can no longer focus on his emotions. They are surging and I want to scream. Aurelia?

Aurelia.

Aurelia is at the bottom of all of this. And she never told anyone? Not when the Scrim came for Sadie two years ago, and not now. Even without anyone knowing his name the second time he appeared, she had to at least suspect. No, she's too smart—she knew. She *knew* but did *nothing* to warn her daughters. Fine, she hates the town and doesn't give a crap about humans, but her own daughters were at risk, again, and she said *nothing*.

She said over and over again that she loves me, even beyond my sisters, as horrible as that was to hear. And I felt her truth, accepted her pain as my own. But what toxic, useless love is it if she'll dangle me to the wolves rather than admit she might have *made a fucking mistake once?*

My thoughts are whirling, twisting in on themselves like a vicious cyclone that will lay waste to everything if I don't shut them off.

So—I choke it all down. Store it away. Hide it. Swallow it. Bury it.

Something tells me it won't stay there, but now is so not the time. Besides, I have done this for so many years it's like second nature.

I force my clenched fists open, my shoulders flat. I swallow until the urge to grind my teeth subsides. Then I reach out and place a hand on his arm. Looking into those beady eyes, I keep mine wide with acceptance and free of judgment. "Will you tell me what happened?"

He looks down at my hand on his arm and then back up at me. "You're nothing like her. But you're just who I thought she was."

I run my hand up his pale hairless arm, the skin reminding me of a salamander's but I don't pull away.

His eyes grow big and wet. "I remember . . . I was in love with her . . . once. Or so I convinced myself at the time."

"My mother?"

He nods. "But it was unrequited and in my youth

I chose the wrong path. I made the wrong decisions. I was so loved here in Brae. All the pixies wanted me." He taps his chest with the arm I'm not rubbing. "Me. They all loved me. I was the most beautiful, the strongest, the wisest. I had the most power, the most charisma, the most . . ." He slips his arm from under my hand and holds both of them out wide. "Everything."

His hands drop heavily to his sides. I suppress a sigh of relief as my hand falls away.

"I could have had my pick of pixies here, and I did. I sampled the females and I tried to find one to settle down with but . . ." He sighs. "They all fell short. None of them was my match and no matter how hard I tried to fall in love, I couldn't. I didn't."

He presses his hands into his knees and stands up. He crosses to the stone railing and looks over.

"I was a world walker back then."

"A world walker?" I stand and move to his side, looking out at the desolate landscape harsh under the newly vibrant green sky. I can't see the cathedral from here or the Nexus.

"It's exactly what it sounds like. I can cross over into other worlds." He huffs out a breath. "Or I could."

His hands clench the natural stone balustrade. He looks down, his gaze unfocused, as if looking inward. He's no longer menacing, just a scared, misunderstood little pixie in a giant's body. Then he looks out again, his gaze scanning the rocks and then the sky.

"Earth was one of my favorite destinations. The exotic food. The beautiful women. The vastness. There were so many places to see and so much to experience."

"It is rich with culture," I agree, mostly to keep him talking.

"When I saw your mother . . ." He turns to me again. "She lit the missing fire inside. I knew in an instant that she was the one I'd always been searching for. The reason no pixie here could tame me. Her wild red hair, her bicolored eyes. The way she loved, deep and fierce. A love I'd never seen before or since."

His eyes grow damp and he looks away but continues a moment later. "I wanted her but she didn't want me, and when I wouldn't take no for an answer," he holds up his arms again, "she turned me into this. She stripped me of my world-walking powers and cursed me to live here as a monster so none of my kind would ever love me again."

Yup, that sounds exactly like Aurelia. The Scrim was another of her victims. And just like that, my heart breaks.

CHAPTER TWENTY

CASPIAN

*D*ominic and I get a ride back to the grove. We run to the tree portal.

"Should we hide in wait or stand out in the open?" All of this planning and we forgot to talk about the moment of truth.

Dominic drops his duty rig loaded with our cop stuff, moving gingerly. What did Aurelia do to him? "Let's shift and wait for Rhys and his ghoul escort. Sorry I didn't think this through. Getting our girl back and dealing with her mother has . . ."

"Taken a strain, man, I get it." I throw some leaves over our stuff and we go off in separate directions to shift.

It's easier for him to blend in, and not for the first time I'm envious of his spider form. It's so darn versatile. My gray fox perches in a branch of the tree while Dom waits next to the portal itself, blending into the trunk.

A few minutes later the ghoul arrives, Rhys in tow, to open the door.

The bedraggled creature stands in front of the tree with Rhys padding almost silently behind him as Botting. He leaps into the branch of another tree.

"Master." The ghoul, who is freakishly tall, calls out with a gravelly voice, his hand firmly grasping the trunk. "We need you."

At first nothing happens and I silently curse but then the bark takes on a spongy appearance and begins to whirl, like the remnants of sludge slipping down a drain. Slowly the speed increases until it's a whirring mass too fast for the eye to capture. Within seconds the portal spins open but instead of the Scrim's face, a hooded human with a large wooden staff stands on the other side. Instead of the portal appearing in the middle of their sky, it looks like he's in a cave. A glossy black cave.

The figure hovers on the other side. "I can't come through, but with Iphigenia and the Scrim both here, I can open this portal."

How dare he speak our girl's name. Who the hell is this guy? I don't wait to find out. Friend or foe, it matters not. I puff out my gray chest, suck in a breath and leap at the man's face, claws out. Knocking him over, he scrabbles back, yanking me off and tossing me to the side. Dominic scurries through and the portal shuts, leaving us shrouded in complete darkness.

Thorn

Squinting into the vibrant green light, I make my way back to the Nexus with Nolan perched on my back. I can't stop thinking about Iphi. The shared intimacy, the love that's blooming. The way the Scrim kidnapped her, the way she went willingly. Still, what's gnawing at me is the way she read my mind. It's one step from reading it to controlling it. I can't handle it, even though I love her and I want to be the fourth man in her life. But I just spent countless weeks stuck in my dragon form against my will, thanks to her mother. And then I get to Brae and bam! The pixies mind nab me. With the return of my free will and my human body,

I should have been safe, but then Iphi does it too? If she truly can't control it or ever learn how to, can I still be around her without literally losing my mind?

Once I'm close to the Nexus, winged creatures take flight and buzz alongside me.

"Thorn? You're enormous. What happened?" Astra buzzes at eyelevel and I have to stop myself from snapping at her. Remembering how she stole my will boils my dragon blood and I close my eye before responding.

I can change sizes but that doesn't matter right now. The Scrim has Iphigenia. She wanted to go with him. But why?

"When you were in Pei, the cathedral city?"

Yes. He plucked her from a tower like a Barbie doll.

"What's a Barbie doll?"

Never mind.

"We warned Taylor against going there, against showing you and the girl where it is. That's where we lived when the Scrim came and . . ." Astra's face pales and Basil flies up next to her.

"What's done is done." She nods and they veer off back toward the encampment below. I follow, Nolan scrambling to stay on my back.

I land far enough away to keep my wings from destroying the beehive of carefully stacked living quarters. Basil, Astra and Bagaata approach. Nolan tumbles off my back and lands in the dirt. He gets up and brushes himself off.

"Wren?" Astra gasps, then lands on Nolan's shoulder.

He bows, keeping his torso steady. "Yes, Mistress Astra, it is I. My name is Nolan."

She takes flight and hovers in front of his face.

"What's this? Why didn't you show us your true form? Deception!" Basil points a tiny finger at him.

"Poshty," exclaims Astra. "Can you blame him? After the way we've treated humans here?"

Basil narrows his eyes. "What are you on about, woman?"

"Well . . ." She bats her lashes at Nolan. "No harm done."

"Are you flirting with him?"

"He *is* quite handsome." She lands on Nolan's shoulder and continues staring openly at him.

Basil lands next to her and puts his arm around her shoulder. "Now, now, *wife*."

"Well he is," she titters and Nolan glows with a smile bright enough to light all of Brae.

Bagaata stays in the air. "Nolan." She inclines her head. "I suspected you were a shifter but I think you made the right decision to stay in your rat form until we truly came to know you. Even if I don't like being lied to."

Nolan tips his head to her. "My apologies, Bagaata."

"Accepted. You're more useful when you're larger anyway." She turns to me. "Where's your girl?"

Captured, by the Scrim.

She shakes her head, black hair swaying. "No surprise if you were with her in Pei."

He destroyed part of the cathedral while we were there and grabbed her off a tower. I'm sorry that part of your city was destroyed. Though come to think of it, hadn't Taylor said the Scrim already destroyed most of it before? I didn't see any signs of that. Perhaps he rebuilt it.

"How was the city?" Bagaata asks.

I work to keep my mind blank but flashes of Iphigenia's creamy skin work its way in.

"Oh!" Astra covers her mouth.

"That's quite enough, Thorn." Bagaata's tone is all school marm.

Then get out of my head, I shoot back.

"He does have a point," says Basil.

Bagaata waves her arm in front of her face. "Never mind. Is there water? Is it safe now or is the Scrim still there?"

I shake my scaled head. *He's gone with our girl but I*

still don't believe it's safe without a dragon escort and two humans. I look around. *Where's Taylor?*

"You didn't see him? He walked there early yesterday morning in case you needed his help. He should have arrived before you left if nothing else held him up."

Taylor went to Pei? Crap, we must have crossed paths, one above and the other below. *We didn't see him. We need to go back.*

Bagaata clucks. "He can take care of himself. He's managed it here for a very long time."

Astra flies off of Nolan's shoulder and moves in front of him again . . . and stares. He smiles at her and holds up a hand, palm up. She lands on it and blinks up at him. Basil snorts and takes to the air, sulking.

We still need to go back. It's the last place we saw Iphigenia. I flap my massive red wings, which undulate under the vibrant green sky. The pixies who had been inching just a bit too close are sent spinning ass over wing, buffeted by the powerful gust. Point made.

"Why would we go back there? It's the site of the pixie massacre," says a young female.

"Listen up." Bagaata uses a commanding voice and everyone stops to listen. "It was always the plan to go back."

"Once the Scrim was gone for good, yes." Basil shoots a sidelong glance at his wife, who's sitting cross-legged on Nolan's open palm now, staring up at him with a smile so wide her teeth sparkle.

Bagaata snaps her fingers and everyone turns to her again, even Basil and Astra. The woman sure has presence. "As Thorn's pointed out, we have his assistance and that of his cousin. The huge dragon alone is enough to defeat this evil once and for all."

"It's too dangerous," says a male pixie clutching his newborn child.

"No one is being forced to go." Bagaata clucks. "But those of you who wish to take our city back, to take our planet back, *now is our chance.*"

The crowd rumbles with discontent. Some agree and others vehemently disagree.

"First," Bagaata says, "I'll go with Thorn and his cousin to scout."

I tap Nolan's shoulder with a wing tip and he jumps, accidentally dislodging Astra from his hand. She tumbles in the air for a moment and then takes flight. Basil joins her, throwing an arm over her shoulder and flaring his nostrils at Nolan, who doesn't notice.

"Sorry, Astra," Nolan says.

"I'm fine." She blinks her eyes at him and Basil stiffens, pulling her in tighter. "Now Basil, you have nothing to worry about. Nolan's simply eye candy. You can't fault me for looking." She kisses her husband on the cheek.

"We need to get you a . . ." Bagaata looks down at Nolan's nakedness. "Covering."

Astra giggles.

"Astra? You and Basil gather a long swath of cloth, please." The sorceress folds her arms over her chest and the two fly off.

After several minutes, during which the pixies continue to argue, Basil and Astra return with a covering, of sorts, for Nolan. He takes it from them with a pained smile and wraps it around his groin, shooting me a look. What did I do? Oh, a small puff of smoke escaped accidentally. Oops.

"That's better," says Bagaata, nodding at Nolan.

"Not in my opinion," mutters Astra.

"Nolan, climb on Thorn's back immediately. We're heading back to Pei," Bagaata commands.

He does as the woman says. Her tone rankles, as does the way she takes over command of *my* plan. For now, though, it's what I want anyway, so I keep quiet. But when I get back to Earth, the first person that orders me to do anything but whatever the hell I want is gonna get a face full of fireball.

Nolan uses my spikes as handholds to climb up my tail and onto my back.

"This is not my favorite way to travel," he grumbles once he's placed himself. "Try to fly in a straight line, please."

I lift off and the four of us fly to Pei. I keep a slow pace for the pixies. It's not far from their makeshift city and as soon as the first spires loom, Astra and Basil flutter ahead in excitement. I'm surprised to see that the tower the Scrim destroyed with his tantrum is back, glittering in the newly formed sun as though it was never shattered at all.

Pei can regenerate?

"Oh yes." Bagaata hovers near my ear. "It's a living creature of sorts. Like the coral you have in your oceans."

When we reach the black glass cathedral, a translucent moat at its foot comes into view. Liquid inside it shimmers pink, magenta and a rich purple. *Is that water?*

"It is," says Bagaata. "It's our fresh water and Pei is replenishing it, slowly bringing our island back."

Island?

"Brae is surrounded by water on all sides."

But what's beyond? Are there other lands?

"Not that we've found."

I land outside of Pei, beyond the moat. The courtyard isn't wide enough to contain me and I don't want to destroy this living structure, not after it's finally started to come back. Bagaata continues on, following Astra and Basil. Nolan slides off my back. But where is Iphigenia? She may not want me to look for her, but I'm tired of taking orders. And it's time Iphi learns I'm not a beast to be tamed.

CHAPTER TWENTY-ONE

IPHIGENIA

I shift my weight next to the Scrim, my feet aching and my throat parched. Now that the storm of my emotions has passed, I'm left hollow—and reminded of how long it's been since I had a decent night's sleep and a nice meal.

Beside me, the Scrim has gone quiet. My newfound sympathy for him is unwelcome to say the least, but as I think of all the people he's hurt in retaliation for Aurelia's actions, all the lives he's ruined, for the first time, I don't feel righteous indignation. I just feel tired. "Do you want to change back?"

"More than anything. That's the only reason I was stalking your world, to try and get your mother to come to Brae and undo what she did to me."

"Why didn't you just take her yourself?"

He runs his other hand along the makeshift stone banister. "I need a touchstone. Your father was that for me for these past years."

"Touchstone . . . you mean an anchor? Like Rhys and Nolan and those ghouls they made to do your bidding?"

He just nods. A good thing, too, since my anger is threatening to bubble up again.

My father was his touchstone, his anchor. Another person my mother "loved" and let be sacrificed. How many years did my father spend a slave to this creature?

I bat the thought away for now, since it's unclear just how much control the Scrim had of himself once Aurelia cursed him. Instead, I turn my thoughts to logistics. "This touchstone slash anchor thing, I don't understand it." I sit down on the rock overhang, running my hands over the smooth surface of the black stone.

"For decades I couldn't leave Brae, but like most things, eventually your mother's spell weakened, or maybe the contingency was always there and it just took a century for me to find another way in."

"The contingency? You mean the anchors?"

"Yes. I could open the portal to your world but not cross over. So everyday I would do so until one day, someone approached."

That someone was probably my father, but the Scrim is having a hard enough time telling this tale. I won't stop to point out just how he ruined my father's life in that moment.

"Once he was close enough for my powers to reach him, I called him to me—and then I reached into his mind." The Scrim sits down, facing me. "I didn't know what would happen but I hoped it would allow me to cross over. And it did, in a way."

I lean forward. "How?"

"Touching him transferred a small portion of my being into him. He was my first anchor. I was able to control him, and using him as a puppet, with a kernel of my consciousness, I was able to cross over to Earth myself, for a short time."

"And so you created more of these puppets? These anchors?"

"I did, drunk on the chance to finally leave my prison, to come to Earth and get revenge on your . . ." He looks away but I understand.

I don't understand his choice to hurt people. There's no excuse for that in my world but I can physically feel the pain he's been in, trapped in a hideous body on a desolate land, barred from his favorite playground for over a century. It'd be enough to drive anyone mad. But I suspect he's not just mad from that.

"All you see is this monster. It's all anyone sees . . . now. But with you here, it's all coming back to me. How I used to be. The integrity I had. And lost."

He's not lying.

"I was loved once." He offers me a wan smile, and yet the sincerity behind it hooks me and draws me in, downward, under wave after wave of pain.

Everything goes black and I reach out to steady myself but I'm no longer sitting on the rock balcony. I'm floating instead and when the blackness dissipates I'm surrounded by the brightest, most lovely sight I've ever seen. The land below is lush with every color imaginable. Green trees grow tall, and grass is dotted with flowers bright with colors found nowhere on earth. The air is filled with tiny pixies, singing and dancing between the blossoms. The glass cathedral towers ahead, but instead of jet-black, it's tall and bright blue, almost cyan. Violet lakes stretch into the distance below an emerald-green sky fading into a pink horizon.

Beside me is a beautiful pixie. His golden hair fans out behind him and his boyish features are open with delight—a chiseled chin and cheekbones, eyes as bright as ferns below flaxen brows, and a perfectly formed mouth cracked in a never-ending smile. Female and male pixies surround him, vying for his attention, and he spends a moment talking to each, dancing with each and flitting alongside each and every one.

"Auberon, pick me," one pixie giggles.

"No, me," says another and they swarm and dart around him.

"I pick all of you," his honeyed voice calls out.

"That's not allowed," says a male pixie. "You have to choose one."

Auberon mock frowns. "Not if that hurts someone's feelings."

The male pixie rolls his crimson eyes. "That's not fair to the rest of us."

"You're right." Auberon stops flying and hovers in the air. The others surround him. "In that case, I pick none."

A collective sigh rains down from the others but Auberon is already flitting away with a handful of pixies chasing after him.

Blackness encloses me once again but this time I welcome it, and when I open my eyes I'm back at the stone fortress, sitting on the overhang with the Scrim next to me. His head is buried in his hands and he's softly sobbing.

I reach out a hand and rub his back but my hand sinks inside, burrowing into his flesh. I gasp. He doesn't seem to notice though, and I pull my hand back out to look at it but there's no blood. If anything, it looks like a ghost hand, completely see-through. Driven by an instinct I can't articulate, I plunge my ghost hand into his back again, feeling around until I find his heart. Then I clutch it and begin an incantation.

"Reducam enim conversionem eorum vera sui, vera sui, vera sui."

At the sound of my voice, the Scrim's body vibrates, slowly at first and then faster and faster until he's practically spinning in place.

"What . . . are you . . . doing?" he asks but it's too late. A loud pop fills the air and his massive form explodes like an oversized helium balloon.

Rhys

*N*ow that Leo the ghoul has done his job and my packmates have gone through, I conk him on the back of his head with a nightstick I borrowed from Thorn's gun belt. Now I have to carry his unconscious body back to the police station. I promised to free his friends if he helped me. And getting Iphi back so she can fix them *is* helping them, so there's no lie there.

Behind the portal tree, its bark no longer swirling, I shift back into my human form without being seen. I carry the bedraggled ghoul to my house to grab some clothes, laying him down on the grass outside. I don't want to stop to dress but it probably won't endear me to show up to the station buck naked.

When I emerge, however, Leo is gone. Crap, he must have come to. I run into Dominic's to snag a few pairs of zip ties, which he always keeps in the same place.

At first I can't find Leo; he's wandered from where I last saw him, but I know where he's headed so I jump into my car and peel out onto the street, heading in the direction of the station. Within minutes I spot him on the side of the road, lurching. He's looking a little worse for wear.

I pull up next to him and roll down my window. "Leo, let me give you a ride."

He jerks his head in my direction, his swollen, bloodshot eyes blinking against the harsh afternoon sun. Leo opens his mouth to speak but all that comes out is a cracked, dry cough. He turns away and keeps lurching forward.

I put the car in park and leap out the door to

wrench his arms behind his back. Slipping the cuffs around his wrists, I pull the plastic straps tight. He wails loudly, flailing.

"Taking you back to your friends, buddy." I steer him toward the car but he bucks and pulls, taking me off-balance.

We face-plant in the dirt on the side of the road. He springs to his feet and runs down the sidewalk with me chasing after him. Comical. For a decaying ghoul, he sure can book it. I still manage to throw my arms around him in a bear hug and twist him around. The short burst of energy apparently wore him out because this time he goes willingly.

As soon as I pull up to the station, I realize I probably should have called this in first. Clenching my jaw, I exit the car, stuff the key card into Leo's pocket and then pull the cuffed ghoul from the back seat. We enter the station.

"Hey, it's Rhys," a deputy calls as soon as I'm inside. "Let go of the ghoul and place your hands on your head."

Not the brightest tool in the shed. Emphasis on *tool*. I'm the one who walked in here, buddy. But he's drawn his weapon so I do as he says.

"Chief, get out here," someone else says into a phone.

"Hands behind your back," Deputy Tool orders,

and I comply, trying not to grunt as he cuffs me too tight.

A female officer hauls the ghoul away, presumably back into the holding cell.

"Rhys." Sheldon emerges from his office. "Follow me." He does a double take when he sees I'm cuffed. "Deputy, uncuff him. He walked himself into the damn station."

Chastened, Deputy Tool removes the cuffs. Sheldon looks like he wants to swat the kid upside the head but refrains.

Once inside his office, the chief motions to the chair in front of his desk and I sit. He drops into his own chair with a sigh.

"I'm not going to give you a lecture, Rhys. You're a good man. You've been training my staff here for the past few months. And I'm guessing you broke the ghoul out in some fool notion to try and save Iphigenia."

I relax.

"But what you did was extremely dangerous and highly illegal, so I will have to punish you."

I look down at my hands folded in my lap.

"Twenty hours of community service. Now," he stands, "how do we get your family back?"

Iphigenia

I collapse from a deep exhaustion, as though I could sleep for a hundred years and still it wouldn't be long enough. My eyes fall closed even though I'm terrified I've accidentally harnessed too much power and killed the Scrim. It's the last thing I ever want to do. Hurting someone would be bad enough. But to kill them? Unforgiveable. I'd rather die. Jumbled thoughts. *Try to open your eyes, Iphi.*

Someone speaks in a melodic voice I don't recognize. "You did something. I don't know what but . . ."

I force my eyes open.

Standing in front of me, looking at his hands, is the Scrim—but not the Scrim. He's shrunk in size, now only six feet tall, and his features have changed to that of the beautiful man from the memory, with golden skin, golden eyes, and long, flowing golden hair. He looks up from his hands, smaller now without claws, and blinks, tears in his sun-kissed eyes. "Are you okay? You look utterly spent."

He's right. I can't even respond but I manage to nod.

Crouching next to me, he picks up a limp hand.

"Bagaata is the only doctor here. I don't want to leave you alone while I get her . . ."

"No, I'm . . . fine." My eyes float shut again. I've never used that much energy, that much power at once. "Just lemme sit."

"If you're sure," his voice wavers.

"What . . . happened?" Was I able to transform him back to his true shape? Reverse my mother's curse?

He squeezes my hand gently. I want to pull it away but I haven't the strength. "This is what I look like, yes, but I'm supposed to be the size of a pixie. If the others see me like this, they'll still be afraid."

I can't help but feel a little of his cautious joy and take pleasure in it. But this is the same being that killed my sisters, my mother's first husband, enslaved my father and destroyed countless lives. All of that is just too unforgiveable, too diabolical.

He lets go of my hand as though he can read my thoughts and not the other way around. "I'm a monster. What I've done is reprehensible. I deserve to roam the violet sea forever."

I have no energy to perform anymore magic but I'm still able to probe, as though it's an inherent part of who I am. In a flash I'm back at my mother's hut with her first family. She's alone, down by a river, washing clothes by hand, smiling and singing. If I weren't witnessing it myself, I'd never have believed this woman is the same one who raised me. There's a carefree joy about her, a spark of delight that I've never before seen or even glimpsed. I watch her through the Scrim's eyes as he perches in a nearby tree.

"I know you're watching me," she says without looking up.

He takes flight and approaches her. She stops what she's doing and holds out a hand, palm down. He lands on top of it, bows low and then kisses it. She giggles like a schoolgirl. "You know this will never work, Auberon."

"Why not?"

"We've been over it before too many times to count. Oh how you try my nerves. We're not the same size, let alone the same species."

"You're married to a human. What does species have to do with anything? And you're a witch. Surely you can cast a spell to make me your size."

She looks down at him and purses her lips. "I can't. I shouldn't."

"You can and you should. How will we ever know if you don't? You've told me you want to be with me. Was that a lie?"

"No. Yes. I don't know." She sighs. "The way you describe Brae and how different everything is there, how accepting the pixies are . . . Of course I dream of leaving the struggles of this world behind but . . ." She shakes her head. "It's just a dream. I could never leave my family."

The Scrim flies off her hand and buzzes around her face. "I'll tell him then. Your husband. I'll tell him how you've flirted with me, how you've led me on, how you've toyed with my heart. I'll tell him and then I'll take you to Brae where you'll see its beauty, forget about them and finally accept our fate. Our destiny."

She holds her hands up. "Please. Don't. I'll do it. I'll change your form, make you my size so we can be together."

Auberon dances around her head.

The memory fades out, another taking its place. It's the night of a full moon in a field surrounded by trees. Mother is there, dressed in a long black dress that cascades behind her in an elaborate train. Auberon sits still on a rock in the center of the field, and they are both surrounded with lit black candles. Even I know this is a bad sign but the little pixie, apparently under the duress of love, obsession or both, doesn't think anything of it. The only thing in his mind is excitement over the impending spell. He believes my mother. He's blinded by a love I can understand because it's the same thing I feel for

Rhys, for Caspian, for Dominic and, now, for Thorn.

Aurelia speaks in an unfamiliar tongue. It's not Latin at first but then she adds to the spell in our witches' tongue. She draws symbols in the air with her athame, and when she chants, her lips move but no words escape. Her hair takes on a redder hue, flying up and around her face, the same way it always does when she performs a powerful spell.

Auberon's eyes are wide, his mouth cracked open, the love in his heart surging out, aimed straight for my mother. The poor creature never stood a chance.

He begins to grow and elongate, just as she promised. His eyes grow wider still and he looks at his hands, his arms, his legs with awe.

"You've done it!" He leaps off the rock and runs toward her, his arms wide, his blond hair whipping behind him.

She holds up one hand and he is stopped dead in his tracks. Her other hand faces the closest tree, and her incantation grows stronger. The bark of the tree morphs and spins.

"No, Aurelia, what are you doing?" Auberon calls.

She turns back to him, her eyes blazing with hatred. "I'm sending you back to where you belong, forever."

As the portal opens, Auberon's form shifts and morphs into that of the Scrim. He screams in pain as his limbs reform, as his face reforms, as his teeth reform.

But from the look on Mother's face, something is wrong, terribly wrong. Magic whips out from her, palpable in its intensity and completely out of control. Her own fear, her own agony has been made manifest, and it's warping the Scrim beyond her original intent.

"Wait!" the Scrim calls as he's sucked toward the spinning vortex.

"I'm sorry." Aurelia's voice is small, all the hatred in her eyes gone, replaced with fear. "I never meant for this to happen. I was only trying to save my family."

Those are the last words he hears as he falls through the portal, back into his own world. A monster.

As the memory fades, I understand. She wasn't apologizing for changing him into a monster on the outside. She was apologizing for changing him into a monster on the inside as well. Without really knowing what she was doing, what she was capable of doing, she removed his free will and his powers and turned the Scrim into a psychopath, a killing machine who had no access to empathy or remorse.

CHAPTER TWENTY-TWO

DOMINIC

*E*ven though I have eight eyes in my spider form, I can't really see in the dark but I can sense vibration and taste the air and other elements in it. This is how I easily locate my brother and scurry onto his back. Foxes can see in the dark and Caspian makes a run for it, weaving through tight corridors and up a slippery ramp into the sunlight.

We pause and blink. Overhead is a bright green sky, but surrounding us are towers of black lava. Where is the hellscape we saw in Chrys's crystal ball?

I can't communicate with my brother but I need him. I'm the GPS and he's my transportation. There's no way I can cross this landscape quickly and neither of us can shift again for another fifteen minutes, or maybe even twenty. I don't want to waste that precious time.

I crawl down Caspian's snout and perch between his eyes, then lift a leg and point in the direction my new radar is pulling me. He bobs his furry gray head. I climb under his neck where there'll be less wind resistance and he takes off. Every mile or so he stops, and I climb back onto his nose to reorient ourselves before he bounds forward again. Finally, we stop at the base of a mountain. At its peak, a large, golden-haired man stands on a rock balcony that juts from the side of the mountain.

Caspian scents the air and in a flash he's off and running up the hill. Without any warning to brace myself, I fly off his fur and sail through the air. Good thing he's a fox and close to the ground. I put my head down and pull my legs in tightly, landing in a soft pile of ash and rolling out of it. I close my eyes and ease into the shifting process, knowing it's time. Over the next several minutes, I shift into my panther, straining to finish as quickly as possible despite the wrenching pain. Iphi is at the top of that hill, I know it. And she needs me.

With four legs instead of eight, I bound up the hill and catch up to Cas, who must have stopped and come to the same conclusion I did because now he's wearing his lion.

When we reach the top, we spot her. Iphigenia looks as though she may collapse. Her head is titled down and she's looking between her hands and this golden-haired man that stands over her. Cas and I creep closer to rest on a rock, just above our girl.

He looks so familiar. Where have I seen those features before?

"Iphigenia," he says with a little twirl, as if he's showing off his body for her benefit. As he turns away from our hiding spot, I see them—wings. And suddenly I know where I've seen those features. Auberon. And the way he looks at her makes me want to rip his giant fairy head off with my teeth. "Thank you for changing me back."

Cas and I exchange a loaded glance. She changed someone? Iphigenia has this kind of power, like that of her mother? Aurelia can look into someone and turn them into their worst nightmare. But this golden-haired man is straight out of a Marvel movie. So Iphigenia can look into someone and, what, see something beautiful? No, he said *changing me back.* So she sees their true self? And then pull that person out, transforms them into who they were meant to be all along.

So who was Auberon before Iphi changed him back? Of course—*the Scrim.*

Iphi sways on her feet and then collapses. The

beast hidden in the golden body of a god licks his lips and takes one step toward our girl. I leap over the rock and snatch the man in my maw, shaking him like a rag doll.

Thorn

I fly around in circles, extending my search wider and wider. I don't want to abandon Nolan and the pixies, which keeps me circling back to them at intervals.

Something in the distance catches my eye and I take off toward it without hesitation. I suck air through my sensitive snout, scenting. Iphigenia. Her scent is unmistakable, light flowers on a warm summer breeze. I must rescue my woman from harm. My huge dragon heart practically vaults out of my chest, spinning like a top. As I close in on her, my fear dissipates. She's sitting atop Dominic in his black panther form, and they're speeding toward Pei. I don't have a moment to wonder how he even got into Brae because on his tail is Caspian in his lion shift, carrying a flaxen-haired giant.

What the hell is going on?

As they near, the scents change, expand, until the air is pungent with fear but it's not Iphi's fear and it's not that of my brothers, so I hover as they pass and then follow behind them to Pei. Dominic barrels toward Nolan, leaps the moat and bounds up a set of stairs into the obsidian cathedral with Caspian following close behind.

I'm too large to follow so I land on the other side of the moat and Nolan stands, waiting with me.

More scents fill the air, cloying in their magnitude. I turn my head and spy thousands of small dots heading our way. The air is filled with them. I crane my head back toward the tower and there at the top of a spire is Iphigenia's whipping hair.

CHAPTER TWENTY-THREE

CASPIAN

*a*t the top of the tallest glass spire, Dominic stops and Iphigenia slips off his back like oil oozing off water. Brae has changed mightily since Iphi's arrival, apparently, given that there were no glass spires and green skies in Chrys's ball so long ago. The spire we've ascended is like something out of a fairy tale, a tall tower in a mighty castle surrounded by a moat. But I'm worried this isn't one of those happy fairy tales, given the whole thing's jet-black. The wide terrace is surrounded by a thick railing, which will hopefully prevent anyone from being pushed off the edge.

Thankfully Auberon lumbers off my back. It took all my will power not to throw him off on the way here. Even though Iphi has assured us that he's under control, I don't like it and I know Dominic doesn't either. It's close to impossible not to see this guy as the enemy, the big bad, the Scrim. The demon that's rained destruction, both on Earth and here in Brae, for decades.

The way he's looking at Iphigenia, who is wobbling on her feet, brings out my inner beast. I growl.

"Scrim!" a booming voice calls out from the top of the staircase. It's the hooded man. The one who opened the portal and I snarl, tossing my head at Dom.

There are just two too many threats up here right now, no matter what Iphi says. Dom must agree because together, we sink into a crouch, our bodies low to the ground, stalking the newcomer in unison so we can pounce together.

The man doesn't seem to notice us. His hood is back, his staff held high, and he's staring at the now-shining Scrim with pure hate.

When we're close enough to pounce, Dom bares his teeth.

"Cas, Dom, no!" Iphi cries out but it's too late.

Dom knocks him down, his big black paws pushing against the thin man's torso. I'm a split second behind, aimed at his legs. He falls with an oomph.

We stand over him, our mouths open, daring him

to fight back. But he doesn't. A trickle of blood drips from the side of his mouth and his unfocused eyes blink wildly. "Please . . ." he rasps. "Take care of my daughter." And then his eyes roll up and his head lolls to the side.

Oh shit, this is Iphi's father? Did we just kill Iphi's father?

Iphi crawls over to us, collapsing next to him, and lays her head on his chest. Then she looks up at us with watery eyes. "He's alive but please, you two —I know you're trying to protect me but when I tell you not to attack someone, you need to listen." Though her tone is kind, her voice is firm.

I lick her face and Dom nudges her father. He moans.

"Daddy?" Iphi's voice is so small, like that of a child.

"Iphigenia." His eyes flutter open and he cups her cheek in one hand. "Your protectors knocked the wind out of me."

"The blood?" She wipes the corner of his mouth.

"Bit my tongue." He manages a chuckle but it's a raspy, ugly sound.

Iphi helps him sit up but his gaze is narrowed, his focus returned to the golden man-beast. "What are you doing with him?" He turns to his daughter.

"Helping him, Dad."

"He's beyond help. That man . . . thing . . . is pure evil."

"No. He's not."

He sighs, the sound somehow indulgent and fatherly all at once. "You see the good in everyone, darling, you always have. Even when it doesn't exist."

Iphi clasps her father's hand. "I can see what's truly inside someone's heart. I've seen pure evil. I've looked into the hearts of men and women for whom there was no salvation. Auberon is not one of those creatures.

"You forget, I've seen him in action. He enslaved me." Her father shoots the former beast another glare.

Iphi squeezes his hand. "When you were under his control, the things you did—were you acting of your own free will?"

Oh shit. My feet go out form under me as I plop down next to her father. Understanding finally dawns.

He softens and nods his head. "Wise girl, beyond your years." He kisses her forehead.

"Dad, I'd like you to officially meet two of my boyfriends. This is Caspian." She kisses my muzzle. "And this is Dominic." She runs her hands down his sleek body. Then her voice chokes, like she's having trouble forming her next words. "Boys, this is my father, Taylor."

Her father stands up, wiping the blood from his mouth on a sleeve, and bends to gather her in his arms.

"Over there, please." She waves toward Auberon, still standing at the railing.

Taylor carries her over but his features are tight, pinched and he throws daggers at the giant boy-man. He sets her down a few feet from him and she leans her back against the black wall of the balustrade. "All of you, please trust me."

Trust her to do what? She can't even walk. The strong, powerful Iphigenia is gone and only a shell remains. It's as though someone pulled the plug at the bottom of the ocean and all of life's water has leaked out. "Auberon won't hurt anyone. I just need . . . to catch my breath."

She does not look like she'll be fine anytime soon. She sags, her head lolling on her neck. What's going on? Why is she so weak?

"I used my powers to change Auberon back." She looks up, her magnificent curls gone limp. Even the shine has dulled.

"I need all three of you on my side with this." She looks between me, Dom and her father, but her eyes are drooping. Then she sags forward, her entire body slipping all the way down.

Dominic springs into action, knocking Auberon down and standing on his chest. His head cranks back in a mighty roar.

"Dominic, no," Iphi murmurs from where she lies. "Please . . ."

His head swings toward her but her eyes remain closed.

"He's trying. Please let him make his amends . . . for me."

Dominic narrows his panther eyes and looks between Iphigenia and Auberon, who remains unmoving below him. It doesn't even seem like the man is breathing, much less trying to get away. Then Dom turns to me and I grunt. I don't want to agree, but Iphi is pleading. And she looks like this may be her final wish before passing out. Her father has gathered her in his arms, cradling her. He brushes her limp hair from her face.

Dom pads forward and rubs his head against Iphi's face but she doesn't move. He licks her cheek and this time she smiles but her eyes remain closed. Taylor pulls her in tighter, whispering in her ear.

Auberon gets to his feet and brushes himself off. "I appreciate the three of you giving me a chance to prove myself."

We're only doing it for our girl, asshole.

Auberon sucks in a breath of air and then steps to the edge of the platform. I raise my front two paws on the banister a few feet away. The throng that was approaching just minutes ago is here. The air swarms with thousands of fairies.

"Pixies, not fairies," Auberon mutters.

Wait, what?

"Ladies and gentlemen," Auberon bellows, "I am here to formally apologize for all of the hardship I have caused each and every one of you. And to Brae." He opens his arms. "I don't expect your forgiveness but I do hope you'll allow me to earn it."

"You're a monster!" one of the fairies—er, pixies yells out in a tiny voice.

"You've destroyed our world," another calls.

"You should be punished," yells a third.

"Severely!" growls a fourth.

And a rain of pebbles flies through the air. Auberon covers his face with his hands but doesn't move. He stands, front and center, while his people pelt him with tiny pebbles. Some of the items they're catapulting at him are glass shards from the cathedral and those stick in his the exposed skin of his arms and hands. And their aim is not as careful as it ought to be, with Iphi practically at his feet.

Thorn appears overhead with Nolan riding on

his back. He reaches one large talon down, opening and closing it in a grabbing motion. Taylor stands with Iphi in his arms, raising her up to the dragon, who grasps her. Dominic and I both leap up and scrabble up his other ginormous claw and onto his back.

Iphi's eyes open, and she's mumbling. "You don't understand. There's no one left here to help him. We have to convince Mom. . . she's the one . . ." And her head lolls again.

There's nothing she can do in the state she's in anyway. We have to get her out of here and find help.

Thorn keeps ascending away from the angry crowd. Auberon looks up, watching us escape. His face is spotted with blood, and more pebbles and shards batter him, but he raises his arms overhead and shouts something.

The pelting stops and a unified gasp fills the air as the pixies, too, all look up—past us. I crane my head upward. There's a large hole in the green sky and Earth's black one peeks through. Nighttime at home, the big dipper a welcome sight.

Thorn veers upward, toward the portal opening in the sky large enough for a dragon to fit through. Iphigenia's eyes flutter open and stay open as she looks up. Her lips part and her face tenses. Thorn is mere feet from the portal and I'm finally letting out a sigh of relief when the dragon lets out a wail.

His talons unclench and he drops our girl.

Dominic

I crane my neck downward and roar as Iphigenia sails through the air, back down into Brae. No. *Iphi*, I scream and bite Thorn's foot, trying to get him to turn back but we're already through the portal. Thorn swoops around to re-enter but it's already closed and he wails again, shooting fire into the sky.

He claws the air where the portal was but nothing remains except the dark blue water of our sea. A minute later he's let Cas and I go to land on the beach. Nolan leaps off his back, all of us making noise at once. The three of us rush back toward the ocean but the portal doesn't reappear. Nothing but the calm, cool water stretches out before us. I run in anyway and flail around, trying to find the doorway.

Thorn's shifting back, and in the controlled part of my mind I know he doesn't want to get caught in the Edge as a dragon, especially now that we're on the force. Large animal shifts without prior authorization is a felony now—thanks to the fucking humans they allowed on the council. My rage boils up to the surface, overpowering my rationality and flooding my veins. I roar and paw the water, making quite a scene and not giving a damn.

Nolan wraps his arms around my furry waist and holds me. "Come on. It's closed. We'll have to find another way."

But Iphigenia is still there. I bellow and try to bite him, finally succumbing to my beast. But I don't care. We just got her back and now we've lost her again? No, *Thorn* lost her. I still, a low growl rolling through my chest. There's prey to hunt.

I rear up and butt Nolan aside. My cousin tumbles onto the sand and I sniff the air. Thorn's hiding, probably because he's naked which is illegal too, and since it's nighttime the only beach goers are usually romantic teens, which is a good reason to hide. Even so, he can't hide from me. Caspian has the same idea and moves next to me. At his moment, we don't need words. He roars, taking off down the beach and I follow right behind him. We round a bend and stop in front of a rock pile. Thorn is standing behind it so only his head pokes out.

"What the hell are you two doing? We need to maintain a low profile."

Caspian and I roar together and leap onto the rocks. Thorn looks incredibly small in his human form. I could snap my jaws over half his face and smash him like the cockroach he is.

I open my gaping maw, displaying my razor fangs, and he holds his hands up. "What the fuck, Dominic? Why are you so angry?"

Caspian opens his mouth in warning too and we snarl and hunch lower on the rock, tensing to pounce.

Thorn's thick eyebrows knit. "Do you two think I dropped Iphigenia on purpose?"

Well yeah, because you did.

"Because I didn't. I would never let her go. I love her!"

Our mouths clamp shut and we freeze.

"Jesus, you all run too fast." Nolan turns the bend and stops short. "Are you two out of your fucking minds? Why do you have Thorn cornered as though he's dinner?"

Cas growls again, but it's a tame sound, one to let everyone know it's his choice he's backing down, no one else's.

I sit on the rock next to Cas and try to look civilized as though a mere minute ago I was not threatening to pop my brother's head like a zit.

"Thank you, Nolan." Thorn stays behind the rock.

"Yeah well, it looks like you were handling it." Nolan removes his loincloth and rips it up into strips, handing one to Thorn before tying one of the strips back over himself again.

Thorn ties the material around his groin and emerges from behind the rocks. "Something made me drop her," Thorn says and just like that, my anger is back.

I leap up and Thorn shies back. I can't say it doesn't feel good to intimidate the big bad of our family, but I stalk behind the rocks and shift back, screaming in agony and not caring a damn bit. When I emerge in my human form, Nolan hands me a dick wrap and I don it, then look at Cas. He follows my lead.

The four of us sit in a semicircle on the warm sand. Four grown men in diapers. Talk about emasculating.

Thorn scrubs his normally bald head, a thicket of new growth now present. "I've never dropped anything or anyone in my entire life. My talons practically lock shut."

Caspian snorts, disbelieving, but I know what

he's saying is true. Iphi must have used her gift of persuasion. I've seen it at work. Not only can she read minds, but if she wants to, she can also control them. Dammit, I promised to keep her secret but how can I? Thorn feels terrible, and Caspian blames Thorn, putting our family at odds because I'm withholding facts.

I clear my throat and the pack turns my way. "It wasn't your fault, Thorn."

"Of course it was his fault, dude. No one else was holding her. She didn't *make* Thorn open his talons and drop her." Caspian's voice is high and tight.

"Actually, she did." Well there it is, can't backpedal now.

"She did what?" Thorn raises a brow.

Sorry, Iphi. "She has the ability to control things."

"What?" Thorn's voice rises an octave.

"People. She has the ability to read minds and, on occasion, make people do things."

"Fucking fuck," Thorn snarls. "After everything we shared. After everything she said to me." Thorn stands up, scrubbing his head again and walking in a tight circle around us. "After her mother controlled me. After Astra controlled me. Now Iphi did too?" He drops into the sand, all his anger expelling in a wave.

"Wait a minute, buddy." Caspian's eyes dart

between us. "What do you mean, after everything you shared?"

He doesn't answer, just looks out over the water.

I crane my head, blinking at the moon, our too-black sky full of empty stars.

After a few minutes he stands back up and rejoins our semicircle. "There are a few things I need to talk to you guys about, but I can't do it without Rhys, so let's walk back to the Grove, shower, change and reconvene."

The jerk is going to make us wait for some full disclosure he's hiding? It'd better be nothing more than he screwed our girl. "Fine." I stand up and start walking. The others trail behind me. We stick to the shoreline until we get to our street and then cut up the road. Luckily, it's late and the streets are empty. We don't bother talking.

After we've showered and changed, everyone meets in the parking lot and crams into my Prius. There's little discussion about where we have to go now; we're all resigned.

Thorn sits in the front passenger seat, looking out the window as I push the button to start up the car. As I turn out of the lot, Thorn sighs, long and deep. "I can't wait any longer, I've got to tell you all . . ."

"Shoot," says Rhys from the back seat.

"Iphi and I . . ." He turns to look out the window. "We've . . ."

"Done it?" asks Caspian. His voice is calm, but there's a twinkle in his eye.

Finally. They've been interested in each other from the start. After all, he made out with her at Promise before either Caspian or I did.

"That's a little crass, but yes, that's part of it."

I shoot my big brother a sidelong glance. Wow, if Thorn thinks that's crass, he's obviously smitten, just like the rest of us.

"Oh, it's like that then?" Rhys can read him too. We all can.

"I'm in love with her." Thorn turns and looks at me and then back at Cas and Rhys.

"For fuck's sake," says Nolan.

"Shut it," Rhys barks.

"Hey man." Caspian leans forward, a smile breaking over his face. "It's no surprise. She's amazing. She's the one."

"Yeah," I add. "We don't blame you."

"Welcome to the Iphi train." Rhys claps him on the shoulder.

"You guys aren't pissed at me? Or jealous or . . . ?"

"Nah, we figured it was just a matter of time." I smirk. "But now . . . her dance card is definitely full."

Thorn's gaze zaps out the window, and he holds

his head a little higher now, but my ears don't miss him expelling a long breath.

It makes perfect sense—to me, anyway. Iphi is such a social creature and truly empathic. She can't contain her love for just one person, she never could. And with us, she won't have to.

CHAPTER TWENTY-FOUR

THORN

*W*e all wear pained expressions as we ring Aurelia's doorbell. Freshly showered and dressed after our quick stop at the Grove, it's time to seriously grovel. The gong sounds loud and ominous and the other four turn around to run.

"Hold your places, men." I puff out my chest, square my shoulders and raise my chin.

"What are you five doing here?" Aurelia's voice rings clear through the still-closed front door.

"We need to speak with you, ma'am," I say. "It's about Iphigenia."

The door opens and Aurelia, who is not a large woman, fills the entire doorway with her presence. Her strawberry-blond hair is loose and wild. Her different-colored eyes are ringed in red and her pale skin is splotchy. So the woman isn't a robot after all.

"Why is she still in Brae while the five of you are here? Who's looking out for her there?" She reaches past me and yanks Dominic inside. The rest of us follow. Nolan, the last one to enter, closes the door. She escorts us, Dominic really, into the living room and motions to the couch and chairs. We all take a seat but she stands in front of the large windows that look out into her yard.

Alistair enters, nods to us and drapes an arm across her shoulders. We all wait, exchanging worried glances until they finally turn to face us. Dominic filled me in on everything he overheard when he was spying on the Scrim and Iphi, that her mother was responsible for this entire mess. This won't be an easy conversation.

"Ma'am," I begin.

She purses her lips but says nothing.

"If you know a way into Brae, now is the time to tell us."

A quick shake of her head. "I don't . . . not really. I could try to do it myself, maybe try using you as an anchor, since you've just been over there, but . . ." She looks away.

The five of us stand at once.

"Let's talk for a minute." I motion to my brethren

and we form a makeshift huddle. "You guys trust me, right?"

"Of course," says Dominic and the others nod.

"Let me handle this then."

"Handle what?" asks Rhys.

"Her." I incline my head in Aurelia's direction.

"Not understanding, bro," says Caspian.

"That's fine, you don't have to understand right now."

"Don't do this on your own," Dominic says.

"I need to. You'll do whatever it takes to get Iphi back, right?"

"Dude, do you even have to ask?" says Caspian.

"Then the four of you go wait in my car or go for a walk or something. I'll text you when I'm done here. Got it?" I know they'll listen. I still hold my alpha card over all of them, though I try not to trot it out anymore except for emergencies.

"Sure, whatever you say." Dominic clips my shoulder and motions the others toward the hallway, then turns back. "Thank you for your time. Aurelia, you're in good hands."

"But . . ." she trails off.

"We'll be right outside." Dominic gives her a curt nod and ushers the pack out.

Alistair stands. "I'll be in our bedroom, Aury. I think this young man needs to talk to you alone."

Aurelia's brows wrinkle as she looks between us but Alistair leaves without waiting for a reply.

I motion to a wingback chair and take a seat on the couch. She follows, sitting across from me stiffly.

She's not going to take this well. I expect her to argue and maybe even throw me out, but it has to be said. "Ma'am." I lean forward and place my elbows on my knees. I need to choose my words carefully so I don't spook her right off her broomstick. "Did you know that when shifters shift, we retain our humanity? We can access all of the instincts and senses of our animal but our thought processes are ninety-nine percent human." I've found it's more understandable to explain things to nonshifters using a percentage.

She crosses her arms over her chest and looks down her pointed nose at me. "That's fascinating, but what's your point?" Her voice is clipped and I can't help but bristle. Sarcasm annoys the dragon out of me.

"Shifters can't normally remain in a shift for longer than twenty-four hours but I know a few who have, in extraordinary circumstances, and they've still retained their humanity."

She taps her fingers against an arm. "So?"

"So . . ." I sit up and mimic her posture—a trick Dom shared with me for interrogating suspects.

Arms, chest. Check. "When you"—*pick your words carefully here, Thorn*—"cast the spell on me that kept me in my dragon form, something changed." I let the last word hang in the air, pausing to hook the witch.

"Changed?" She cocks her head.

Bait swallowed. "I'm sure the change wasn't your intention."

"What change are you talking about?" Her arms uncross and mine follow but I do not want her to tweak to my mirroring thing, so I place both hands next to me on the couch. She keeps hers in her lap.

"I became a dragon. *One hundred* percent." I let that sink in for a moment while she considers. "Every day I lost more and more of my humanity. I lost part of my human memories. I started thinking like a dragon thinks."

She leans forward. "What are you saying?"

I hold my hands out. "Your transmogrification spells actually transform a person from the inside out. Personality and all."

"My spell changed your *thoughts*?"

"It did. Without a doubt it did."

She nods, visibly shaken.

But the Aurelia I know wouldn't care so much. Unless her fear is about something else entirely. Come to think of it, she's accepting this way too easily. Almost like she expected it.

"All right, I never meant to do that. It wasn't my intention when I cast that spell but I could see how," she shrugs, "that might happen. By accident, of course."

"Of course." I flash a tight-lipped smile. "I believe that your magic is more powerful than you know."

"Could be." She taps a finger against her arm, looking all over the room, everywhere but at me. "And?"

"And, when you changed Auberon—"

She leaps up, her face going white. "It wasn't just his outside?"

I stay seated, my movements slow so I won't risk startling her even more. "Your spell changed his outside into a monster, and his brain followed."

"Oh no!" She collapses back into the chair, her head in her hands. "That means I'm responsible for the deaths of my own children and my husband? In trying to save them, I *condemned* them?"

She wails as Alistair flies down the hallway and into the living room.

"Aury, what's happened?" He drops to her side, cradling her in his arms.

Iphigenia

. . .

*T*his time, my fall back to the hard surface of Brae is different. No hurtling through decaying darkness and a pile of acrid ash. Now I float back down, like a balloon with a slow leak, and when I land, the pixies surround me, all babbling at once.

Bagaata flies forward. "What were you thinking, leaving your world for ours and standing up for that monster?" She motions toward the cathedral and I chance a look. Neither Auberon nor my father are standing at the top of the tower anymore.

I settle down cross-legged on the soft dirt—and it *is* dirt, not ash. Larger bits of greenery are poking through everywhere. Some have even grown into small bushes and flowers. I motion around me. "What happened to Auberon is not all his fault."

"How so?" Bagaata lands on my knee. Astra and Basil perch on my other knee as other pixies swarm around me.

"My mother is a powerful witch, and over a hundred years ago she changed him into a monster."

Bagaata nods. "We know this but it was because he killed her children and husband."

"Yes, it's true. The children and her husband both accidentally died here but he took them *after* she cursed him, not before. When she cast that spell, it warped not only his body, but his mind as well."

"Meaning?"

"He was no longer Auberon. He became the monster my mother cursed him to become, body, mind and soul."

"He doesn't remember doing it?"

If only. "He does but at the time he had no memory of being Auberon, and he had no remorse or empathy while he was the Scrim. Think about it. He even had a different name. He was, for all intents and purposes, a completely different creature."

The pixies bicker amongst themselves, arguments flying fast and furious.

"And how do you know this isn't just another lie?" Bagaata asks after shushing the crowd.

"Because I can see into his heart." I raise my chin and look into her tiny eyes.

"What poshty," says a teenage pixie.

"And his mind," I add. That probably makes more sense to them.

"What am I thinking right now?" asks the teen, his hands planted on his hips.

"That wouldn't be hard for anyone to figure out, Timon," says Bagaata. "What about me, what am I thinking?" She closes her eyes and drops her head to her chest.

I send out my probing threads. The woman holds a painful secret. I watch her memory, the one she accessed because it's the only thing she's never told a single soul. A miscarriage when no one, not even the father, knew she was pregnant. She flies close to my mouth and I turn my head to whisper into her ear. "I'm so sorry you lost her."

She pulls in a sharp intake of breath, her glossy eyes looking up. "It's true, she speaks the truth."

The crowd starts murmuring again, the anger lessening as confusion takes hold.

"So all should be forgiven because Auberon wasn't in his right mind?" asks Basil.

"No way," adds Astra. "Look at what he did to our world."

"But look what he's doing now," I counter, spreading my arms wide. "The plants are regrowing, the flowers are blooming, the sky has cleared with no more endless brown dusk or pitch-black nights, and the waters are flowing once again in the rivers, streams, lakes and ocean.

"Too little, too late," Astra grumbles and she's right, I can understand their pain as clearly as I can understand his.

"How can we forgive or trust the monster that almost killed our entire civilization?" Astra peers up at me.

"There's a difference between forgiveness and acceptance. Maybe you could work on the latter and let him make the effort to earn your trust back. To prove himself."

"Did your mother create this evil monster on purpose? To destroy Brae?" asks Timon.

I sigh. "No. It was an accident. She just wanted him to leave her and her family alone but he was smitten."

"More like obsessed," snorts Astra.

She's not wrong. Astra is smitten with Nolan but she wouldn't leave Basil or Brae to have him. "You're right. He was obsessed and my mother was young. She didn't know how powerful she was." I must have inherited a version of that particular power from her. But where she can yank out someone's evil nature, I can tease out their goodness. "She had never cast a spell like that before, and in her anger she damned him."

Bagaata flies next to my head. "We'll take what you've said into consideration, discuss our feelings and then take a vote."

A vote? How . . . refreshingly democratic. "What happens if you vote no?"

"He'll be sentenced to death."

Then again . . .

CHAPTER TWENTY-FIVE

"What did I do?" Aurelia's tears are real. The ice witch has a heart after all. "What can I do to make it right?"

Alistair coddles her and she weeps into his shoulder.

I stand up and kneel next to her chair on the other side. "Please don't blame yourself. How were you to know?"

"I didn't know," she wails.

"Of course you didn't, darling." Alistair pats her head and then gives me a *what the hell is going on* look.

I give him a quick headshake; the last thing the woman can endure is a rehash of events. Someone will have to catch Alistair up later. "You can make this right and you can save your daughter in the process."

She lifts her tear-stained face. "How?"

I repeat my question from earlier, the one she didn't answer. "Can you get us into Brae?"

She tips her head back, looking up at the ceiling and then over to me. "I don't know. But I want to try."

Iphigenia

I wait with Auberon, who is sitting at the top of the cathedral with his bronzed knees pulled up to his chest. Dad stands to the side. I know he's upset that I'm still here but he's giving me a moment of space.

I put my hand on Auberon's shoulder. "How many times have they voted for death?"

He shakes his golden head of hair. "Just once, for me, when I was the Scrim. But I overpowered them and turned their land to dust. It was pure malice. I would have destroyed Brae anyway. How could I have been that evil monster? I'll never forgive myself, and I have no idea why anyone else would. I despise the monster I became. I despise myself even now. Especially now." He drops his head down to his knees.

"You weren't in your right mind. You were a monster, uncontrolled and uncontrollable. But now you're back and surely they'll see that."

Dad comes over. "If they could forgive me . . ."

"Maybe." Auberon lifts his head up, looking back and forth between us. "But I have the memories of what I did as the Scrim. I don't know if I can go on with that knowledge. I don't know if I *want* to go on."

"Did you," I lick my lips, preparing for the answer, "kill anyone?"

He can't meet my eye. "I may not have crushed them with my own hands but yes, a great many died because of what I did both here on Brae *and* on Earth." He looks down at his hands. "I deserve to die. I'm going to tell them so. They don't need to vote." He stands and I stand too.

"If you deserve to die, then so do I," Dad says.

Alarm shoots through me at my father's words and the waves of desolation emanating from Auberon. "Neither of you deserve to die. You both deserve another chance. The pixies already gave you one, Dad." Then I turn to Auberon. "You deserve to turn this around. You need to make good where you previously wronged them. Can you restore Brae completely?"

"I think so." He looks at me, his golden eyes glimmering with the start of something other than despair for the first time since our talk on the mountaintop. "I think that being near you has been recreating it all along."

"Me?"

Dad puts his arm around my shoulder. "You've always been special, attuned to nature and all its creatures, great and small."

It's true. Maybe that connection isn't so passive or one-way. Do I draw my powers from other people? Do I need the lifeblood of nature around me in order to use them? That would explain why my powers were so weak when I got here, why I was unable to read anyone's thoughts until after life started returning to Brae.

I peek out over the wall. Flora is sprouting and growing where there was none before, but the majority of the landscape is still dirt.

"Let's try together." I reach for his hand and Dad removes his arm from my shoulder, moving to the banister to peek over.

We intertwine our fingers and a surge of magic flows through his arm into me. My hair flutters in a breeze that touches no one else, swirling around my face and head. The sensation is not unpleasant but the unknown is a little scary. But Auberon's thoughts, so potent through our connection, are all for the restoration of Brae. His mind's eye is focused on the way it looked before the destruction and I can't help sharing the image, a land filled with greenery, exploding color and magic. I close my eyes and paint the landscape with my mind, letting his energy fill me up.

After several minutes, Dad gasps and Auberon lets go of my hand. The intensity of the magic flowing through me fades as well and I open my eyes. Stretching out before us as far as I can see is Auberon's world, reborn. And we created it together.

CHAPTER TWENTY-SIX

IPHIGENIA

agaata appears, hovering in front of us. "If you did this hoping to affect our vote—"

"I didn't," he interrupts her. "I deserve to die for what I've done."

"Well then, we're all in agreement," she says.

"What?" I whirl away from the view. "No. Please. Punish him some other way. Condemn him to years of hard labor, make him cook and clean or lock him up for a while. Anything but death. On Earth we try to rehabilitate those who break the law, especially if they're remorseful, and he is."

"On Earth you have the death sentence." Bagaata levels her gaze with mine, hovering in front of my face.

"But not everyone believes in it," I counter. "It's not humane."

"We're not human. The vote is final," Bagaata intones.

"I accept my fate."

Dad skirts to my side, still silent, watching the exchange.

Auberon moves toward the edge, then turns and looks at Bagaata. "If I have your blessing, I'll jump from here."

She nods once.

"No, wait!" I scream and reach for him, Dad not trying to stop me, but Auberon's already flung himself off the tower. I rush to the edge and look over the side. Surely the weird way I floated down was Brae's magic and not my own, but no, Auberon is plummeting fast toward the ground. Dad grabs my hand and I hold on tightly, not wanting to watch the death but unable to look away.

Just when I've lost all hope, a thunderclap booms overhead and Auberon freezes in midair, his face inches from the ground. He hovers there, and after a stunned silence, the pixies pelt him with pebbles and stones once more. Above me a hole has opened, and descending through it is—Thorn carrying my mother on his dragon back?

If I wasn't seeing it with my own eyes, there is

absolutely no way I'd believe it. But the sharp intake of breath from Dad at my side confirms that this is oh so real.

"Stop," Mom calls out as Thorn banks through the sky. She looks like a warrior goddess riding a mighty beast, her posture ramrod straight, her beautiful hair streaming behind her like a pennant. She's wearing a long white dress and her eyes are sharp with determination. My heart ripples in my chest with love and admiration. She actually came into Brae atop my boyfriend to save the creature she damned so long ago.

"Aurelia." Dad's voice is a whisper.

The pixies stop throwing the rocks and back away from Auberon, who was taking the beating without covering his face. Blood stains his face and clothes. Mom holds out a hand and floats him to the ground.

Thorn swoops down and lands on the other side of the moat, stretching his wing across it to form a bridge. Mom stands, majestic and proud, holding herself aloft as she crosses. One hand flutters, as if to steady herself. No one utters a sound and the swarm of pixies part for her. When she steps off Thorn's outstretched wing, he turns his head toward me and winks.

Really?

Aurelia stands before Auberon, who won't meet her eye. When she speaks, it's loud enough for everyone to hear.

"Auberon. I can't take back the past but I can affect the future. What I did to you is unforgiveable. Horrible. Changing you into the Scrim was a mistake. Not only did the punishment far outweigh the lack of crime, my spell proved far more powerful than I ever knew. I don't expect you to forgive me but I do hope I can somehow make it right." With a flourish of her hand she closes her eyes. *"Haec est forma reddens."*

A loud bang, like a cannon shot, echoes throughout the valley, and hovering in front of my mother is a pixie-sized Auberon. He's the most ethereal being I've ever seen. His light is so bright, it radiates a foot in every direction.

"What did you do?" Auberon's voice is warm, resonating with a melodic harmony that trails through the air, pulsating and winding, coiling and throbbing like a separate being.

The pixies hum and buzz around him, keeping their distance.

"The Scrim," Mom turns to address the crowd, "was my fault. I condemned this pixie to a fate worse than a thousand years of servitude. Worse than being buried alive. Worse than watching the woman he loved belong to another."

She turns back to him, her voice lowering but still loud enough for all to hear.

"I was the monster, not him."

Iphigenia

*B*efore I can speak to Mom, Dad approaches us. As soon as she sees him, her breath catches.

"I'll let you two talk." I turn to leave.

"Please, stay." Mom's voice is curt, her wall firmly in place once again.

The others move away, leaving the three of us. Dad looks at his feet and then back at Mom.

"I've made a lot of mistakes, Aurelia." He wrings his hands.

"That's an understatement," she huffs.

"I don't expect you to forgive me."

"Good, because that's not going to happen."

He inclines his head and then looks over at me.

"I'm also not going to belabor the past or why I chose to do what I did."

She crosses her arms over her chest and raises her chin. The woman has mastered looking down at people who are taller than she is, and Dad shifts uncomfortably.

"What I do need to say is this." He stares directly into her bicolored, angry, unforgiving eyes. "I truly loved you. More than I've ever loved anyone, with the exception of our daughters."

She gives him a quick nod but the expression on her face remains unreadable.

"My greatest accomplishment is the raising of our children, as much as I was able to be a part of that."

She snorts.

"I don't regret sacrificing my life for any of you. It's the other decision I'm most proud of."

"Daddy." I touch his arm.

"Pumpkin," he turns to me. "I love you so much. I've always loved you and your sisters and I always will. No matter what."

"I love you too."

He gathers me in his arms.

"I don't love you," Mom snaps. "And I don't forgive you."

Dad's lips tighten, a muscle twitching in his jaw.

"But I do understand why you did what you did."
She uncrosses her arms.

His lips twitch.

And that's all she says before she turns and gives
him her back. Dad releases a breath and I hug him
tighter.

CHAPTER TWENTY-SEVEN

THORN

The pixies confer in the cathedral and I wait with Auberon in silence. Iphigenia, who appears to be acting as a mediator for Aurelia and Taylor, approaches with her mother.

She stands so close to me that the heat of her body lights a fire inside mine, then she places a hand on my thickly scaled hide and leans into me. I love being her crutch, though I know she doesn't truly need one.

She clears her throat. "Mama, what made you come back here to help Auberon?"

"Your boyfriend made me want to come back." Her voice sounds neutral, matter-of-fact, with no hint of the anger or the thinly disguised disgust that I'm used to hearing. "Thorn loves you. Your other boyfriends love you and I love you." Her eyelashes flutter. "I know a mother isn't supposed to have a favorite but I did."

"Oh Mama, it's okay. No one has to know." She offers her mother a beatific smile but the older woman's mask is back in place.

"No one ever will." She rests a hand on her hip.

They'd have to be blind and stupid not to figure that out. For as long as I've known Iphi, her sisters haven't even been allowed inside Aurelia's house.

Auberon clears his throat and moves off my shoulder to hover in front of his unrequited love. She holds out a hand and he lands on it, bowing. "It's my turn to apologize, Aurelia. What the pixies decide matters not. What does matter is the way I relentlessly pursued you, regardless of your stated wishes and your obvious love for your family."

Iphi's father inches close enough to listen but remains behind Aurelia, beyond her line of sight.

Auberon continues, "How I threatened to lie to your family. How I killed your family. My actions are unforgiveable and you acted accordingly. I deserved to be trapped in the body of a monster. I only wish I'd maintained my humanity and not wreaked death and destruction on so many." He sits on the palm of her hand and shakes his head. "I ask that you end this here and now. Close your hand and smother me. Slap your other hand flat over this one and smash me. I deserve no less."

Iphigenia gasps, stepping away from me. "Don't you dare!"

"Child," Aurelia peers at her daughter, "do you really think I'm capable of murder?"

Auberon looks like he's swallowed a tree branch.

I flap my wings to draw their attention and crane my neck up. Bagaata approaches from above, landing on my head. *What am I, a podium? Thanks, lady.*

"I can hear you." She pats me.

Whatever.

"Auberon, come here." Bagaata motions to the air in front of her and the pixie leaves Aurelia's palm and hovers where he's told to. "Instead of the assembly deciding, everyone had a say."

Auberon flinches. "Honestly, Bagaata, before you tell me what they've decided, I really don't deserve to live."

"Dying, my dear Auberon, would not make up for all your crimes, now would it?"

"I . . . I don't understand."

"If you're dead, there's no real justice." She pats my head and he lands next to her.

The tiny things tickle my skull and I bite back the urge to toss them off.

"We want you to work, to grow our community, our world and our sense of purpose. To restore what you took from us as best you can. It'll take a long time. Years, probably. But then justice will be served."

Auberon says nothing but as his tiny feet pace on my head, I have to bury the desire to spit fire.

Finally, he comes to a halt. "I don't know . . ."

Iphi's father steps forward, maneuvering around his ex-wife. "What if I help?"

"What?" Iphi rushes to his side.

"I've been in Brae for a very long time and I'd like to help restore it. I, too, need to pay penance for my sins." He glances at his daughter and his eyes soften with affection. "It doesn't have to be forever, but I don't think your mother is anywhere near ready to welcome me back on Earth."

"You've got that right." A line knits between her brow.

"I'd like to stay in Brae," he addresses Bagaata, "and help Auberon rebuild."

The tiny pixie in charge fixes her gaze on Taylor, then Auberon. "Fine, but if either one of you show any signs of malice to anyone, we'll come up with a very painful and very harsh punishment indeed."

The man and the pixie exchange looks before nodding in unison, the bargain struck.

"Thank you, Bagaata." Iphi looks at her father, her eyes glistening.

Bagaata flies off my head, thank the stars, and joins mother and daughter, Auberon in tow.

"You're the one who deserves a thank-you." She smiles at Iphi and then turns midair and glares at Aurelia. "You, on the other hand, have done more than enough damage."

Aurelia sniffs once but otherwise accepts the verbal blow.

Bagaata twirls over to me once more. "Thorn, you've been a hero to all, but now it's time to take care of your girl. And please," she flies close to my ear, "get everyone out of here now."

Iphigenia

Kissing and hugging Dad goodbye is not easy, but just as he's allowed me to make my own decisions, I have to do the same for him.

"Tell your sisters that I love them. Tell them I'm safe and I promise to return when I can." He cups my cheek for several seconds and then lets go. "Climb onto the dragon's back now."

I do as he says, positioning myself in front of Mom.

The portal shimmers and spins above us. Thorn rises, flapping his giant wings and sailing through the air toward it, Mom clutching my waist. We pop out of the portal into the forest near the Grove and though I know that tree trunk was not large enough to fit a giant dragon through it, I have no time to wonder about the hows or whys.

He lands and lets us climb off his back into the darkness. I blink, looking around, but the forest fills with the sounds of shuffling and before I can reach for Mom, we're surrounded by ghouls.

"Can you help us?" one asks.

Mom bristles and pulls me behind her. But no one attacks or comes too close. They watch me with unblinking eyes.

"It's all right, Mom. I think I can help them."

"Over my—"

Thorn reaches out a wing and shuffles Mom toward him. Then he nuzzles her with the tip of his giant mouth. Too weird, but it works. She holds on to one of his spikes and whispers something in his ear. He nods and lets out a puff of smoke.

I can only imagine what she said. Ignoring my

fierce protectors, I motion for the ghouls to come closer. They shuffle toward me.

"Every one of you has to touch me, just a hand." Their stench is ripe but I don't shrink away. Instead, the light I carry inside me from Brae shoots through my pores until I glow as bright as a small sun. The ghouls jump back and some cover their eyes. "You have to touch me for this to work."

"You're on fire!" One of them backs farther away.

"Blazing," another says, this one taking a step forward, eyes wide.

"It's not fire, it's light and it will help heal you. All of you."

I hold out my arms and they inch closer, reaching their hands toward me. When each one is touching me, some with only the tip of a finger, I shoot tendrils of my magic out into each one's heart. I locate the spark in each that made them who they were before they were blighted. I latch onto it and tease it out, feeding it with magic so it grows and grows. I have to focus, searching deep into so many souls at once, but one by one I pull their true selves back into their bodies. That's what I did before with the other ghouls, what I did with the Scrim, even when I didn't know what I was doing at the time. Transmogrification.

Like mother, like daughter.

One by one they let go and fall to the ground, and when the last one disconnects, I open my eyes. I am surrounded by humans—and one vampire—all rubbing their eyes and attempting to stand. I help each one up. Mom and Thorn watch and wait, and for that I'm grateful. I know it can't be easy for either one of them.

"Thank you." A young man who looks to be eighteen takes my hand in his and shakes it. "You saved us when no one else could."

Another steps forward and shakes my hand. "Our savior."

I ignore his misappropriated sentiment. "Do you have somewhere to go?" I ask them and a few shake their heads.

"Most of us have homes and families but not everyone," says the young man.

"Follow us." I look at Mom and Thorn. Aurelia comes up to me and takes my hand. We all walk back to the Grove together.

"I'm proud of you," she whispers in my ear.

CHAPTER TWENTY-EIGHT

IPHIGENIA

hen we arrive, the lights in Caspian's house are blazing and I knock on the door. He flings it open and grabs me, hugging me tightly and burying his face in my hair.

"Iphigenia, you're here? You're really here?"

The other men pile in behind him. "It's Iphi?" asks Dominic. "Let us see her."

Caspian lets go and walks out as the men behind him push forward. "Thorn, buddy!" he cries. "And Mama?"

Aurelia snorts but one side of her mouth quirks up—for a fraction of a second, anyway.

Dominic and Rhys burst through the door. Rhys kisses me hard on the lips. Dominic cups my face in his hands and caresses my cheek. Nolan follows last and hugs me. Then each one hugs Mom and she actually lets them, even if she makes zero effort to hug them back.

When they turn to look at Thorn, they spot the milling humans who followed us here, waiting on the grass.

"Are those ghouls?" Rhys narrows his eyes and puffs out his chest, taking a menacing step forward.

"Not anymore. They're healed but can you guys help me take them home?"

"Of course," Dominic says.

"There are a couple who don't have anyplace to go yet. Maybe they can stay here for the night and we'll figure something out tomorrow?" I look between each of my men and their hard faces soften.

"They can stay at Rhys's with me," says Nolan, looking at Rhys for confirmation. Rhys nods.

"I'll drive your mother home." Caspian holds his hand out and Aurelia takes it.

"Thank you, Caspian." She turns to leave with him.

"Somebody call Sheldon!" Cas calls over his shoulder.

Dominic turns to Thorn and scratches a spot just behind his ear. "Thorn, you go change back, buddy, and then come back over, okay?"

Thorn expels a long, thin line of fire into the air, like fireworks, then saunters off into the woods.

Dominic throws his arm around me. "Come inside?" He gestures into Caspian's hobbit house.

"We'll take the ghouls home and put the others at my house," says Rhys. "Don't go anywhere, we'll be back soon."

"We'll be here. Promise."

Thorn

I'm a bundle of nerves when I knock on my brother's door. It flies open and Iphi stands in front of me wearing nothing but a towel and a grin brighter than the midday Southern California sun in July. Her eyes roam hungrily over my body and even though the evening air is cooling down, my naked skin heats with beads of sweat. One of her long, toned arms snakes out and grabs mine, yanking me inside and slamming the door behind me.

"Hey man." Dom juts his chin toward me. "Wanna jump in the shower? We'll wait for you."

My eyes widen. He catches my look and winks, then walks over to Iphi from behind. His arms reach around her and he loosens her towel. She lets out the sexiest little moan and leans her head on his shoulder as he drops the towel to her feet. I lick my lips, unable to look away. Dominic runs his index fingers down her still-damp skin and goose bumps rise to greet them. She keeps her eyes on me and shivers. My cock doesn't care that I need a shower and springs to full attention, slapping almost painfully against my taut stomach. Her eyes drop, watching it and she sucks in her bottom lip.

Dominic is watching her watching me. His eyes travel down her body as he cups her breasts, one in each hand, and brushes a thumb over her very peaked nipples. She gasps and her lids flutter but she doesn't take her eyes off of me. My erection pulses so hard it aches and without thinking, I grab it.

"Yes," she hisses. I pump myself, watching Dominic play with her. His hands roam over her curves, tracing the outline of her waist, her hips and then settling on the insides of her thighs. Her breath catches and so does mine when he widens her stance, just a little. She leans her body into him and he rubs himself against her. "Stroke it," she growls at me and I do with renewed vigor, surprised that I'd lost my focus watching her.

My cock twitches in response and Dominic spreads her glistening pussy open. Some of her heat drips down the insides of her thigh and all I want to do is drop to my knees and lick it off.

"Keep stroking," she says and I want to please my lady so I do.

I use the drops of pre-come to spread back over my shaft and groan as the head of my dick pulsates under her watchful gaze.

Dom pushes one of his long thumbs up inside of her wet snatch and pinches her clit with his other hand. Her breasts heave and she shudders against him. He rocks into her from behind, his head still dipped down, watching her body. And her eyes are still glued to me. Her hips move and she fucks Dominic's fingers and I don't need to second-guess any of this. My nerves about fitting in or being a fifth wheel are gone. The only thing hammering through my veins right now is lust for this woman, and a big part of that lust is spurred on by watching someone else playing with her her. Not just someone, I remind myself, my pack.

Iphigenia's gaze moves between my own and my throbbing dick, so fucking hard she could use it as a trapeze bar. She moves her own hands up and cups her tits, squeezing them and I almost shoot my wad. This woman is crazy fucking sexy and I can't hold out much longer but I want her to come first. I need her to come first.

She cries out as Dominic buries more fingers inside of her dripping pussy. Opening her legs wider. she bucks against him, holding my gaze and sucking her plump, swollen lips into her mouth. He works her cunt expertly with his hands and I can't look away. I pump my cock harder and grasp my balls with my other hand, tugging and squeezing.

Iphi groans, pinching her own nipples, watching me yank myself. My hand moves harder, faster, keeping up with the friction Dominic is building between her legs.

The moment before I step off the ledge, she screams, "Now, come with me now!" And I do, the heat of my orgasm tearing through my body like molten lead and spurting out of my dick like my breath of fire. Iphi cries out too, bucking and writhing while Dominic moves one hand around her waist to hold her up but keeps his other one working between her legs. Her gaze is still pinned on me as we both come down. She shudders and I lose my balance completely and reach for the wall. Dominic moves his hands to her shoulders, making sure she doesn't fall and walking her over to me, depositing her into my arms.

I wrap her up and kiss the top of her head, her arms wending around my waist, her gaze wandering up to my eyes. A crooked, sly smile plays on her lips.

"I love you, Iphigenia Holt." I lean down and take her mouth in mine, walking backward with her wrapped around my midsection. My hand juts out to push open the bathroom door and once inside, she slams it and into the shower we go. As one.

Rhys

I push open Dominic's front door to the sound of running water. Caspian pushes in behind me. "She's in the shower?"

I shrug, closing the door. Caspian walks to the bathroom door and puts his ear against it, pulling back with wide eyes. "Not just her, man."

"Knock."

He does.

"Come in." Iphi's voice sounds too far away through that barrier.

Cas hesitates, so I barge over and open the door. I'm met with a lovely sight. Dominic has the best shower—a tub really, with room for three—and they're taking advantage of it for sure. The vinyl shower curtain is clear and I stand with my mouth hanging open, watching Thorn and Dom soap her up. Thorn is riveted by her breasts and from the look of it, they must be very dirty. Dominic is positioned at her feet, running his hands along the insides of both thighs and up to the lips of her pink pussy. Her head is back, mouth open, the water dripping down her face and neck. Those blond ringlets are loose, heavy with water.

"Oh my God," Caspian breathes behind me. "Get in there."

I enter the bathroom with Cas on my heels.

My jeans are tight and I want to strip them off but if I look away, even for a second, I may miss something delicious. I reach into my pants and adjust my engorged cock, never taking my eyes off our girl.

Iphi tilts her head back down, opens her eyes and smiles, crooking a finger at us. We walk toward her, hypnotized, and stop right outside the curtain. Thorn and Dom, the good boys, stay on task. Thorn reaches up and unhooks the shower nozzle, aiming the spray at her tits and washing the soap down her luscious body. Dominic helps by wiping suds down her waist and belly in a sweeping motion. They exchange places and Thorn kneels at her feet, aiming the water spray at her swollen pussy. She lets out the sexiest moan and gasps when he inserts a finger, then two. Dominic winds his body behind her but they keep her facing forward so we can watch. He puts one hand on her neck, tilting it back, and kisses her.

Thorn moves the spray up and down her inner thighs, still pumping her with his fingers. A second later he's handed the spray nozzle to Dom, whose hand is reaching down for it, and Thorn buries his face in her pussy. I groan, imagining her taste filling his mouth. I want her on my lips. I want her to come down my throat. Thorn pumps her with his fingers and licks her while Dom kisses her, using the spray on her backside. She juts out her ass and groans louder. Dominic slips one hand down and out of sight.

"Do you want me to play with your ass?"

"Yes, please," she moans.

Dom hands the spray back to Thorn, who backs his face out of her crease and uses the jet on her clit.

I can't see what Dom is doing behind her, but her groans increase and she pumps her hips back and forth, like she's fucking them both.

I squeeze my hard cock through my jeans. No amount of adjusting will relieve this ache. Dominic slides behind her, kissing her neck and widening his stance. A second later the head of his cock appears between her legs. Thorn keeps the spray there but removes his fingers, and Dom's cock slips between her pussy lips and disappears.

Cas and I watch them fuck and when I can't handle it anymore I pull out my cock and give it a few strokes. Thorn runs his hand up and down her legs, keeping the spray of water focused on her clit, and after another minute both Iphi and Dom climax. Iphi bucks and screams while Dom holds her up, pumping hard into her. Her eyes open and she stares straight at me as she comes. It's the most beautiful sight I've ever beheld.

Thorn rinses her sodden cunt with the water stream and she giggles, a delightful sound. He hooks the nozzle back into place above and Dom moves out of the shower. I hand him a towel and he wraps himself up in it. Iphi sits down in the tub and motions for me and Cas. We don't have to be told twice. In record time we're both naked. My throbbing cock pulses against my stomach as I trade places with Thorn. Iphi stands up again, kisses me hard, wrapping her arms around me with her hands moving down to squeeze my ass and then my balls from underneath. Caspian steps in and she stops kissing me to kiss him, her body welcoming us both. One of her hands grabs my cock and pulses, moving up and down on my shaft, then over the head with her thumb. When she steps away from Cas, I lean down to suck her tits.

Those hard pink nipples beg for my tongue and I swirl it around while reaching down between her legs to find Caspian's hand already there, hard at work. I join in. He pinches her clit and I curve my fingers up inside of her. She has one hand pumping me and the other working on Caspian. She leans back into the wall and raises a leg, resting it on the edge of the porcelain tub. Better access. We keep up our ministrations. All three of us, working together in the same rhythm.

Outside the shower, Thorn and Dom are watching. Thorn sits atop his towel on the closed toilet while Dom is perched on the sink, his towel at his feet. They're both playing with their cocks, eyes trained on Iphigenia, and I don't blame them.

She expertly pumps the both of us, looking between the four of us with half-lidded eyes. Cas and I work as a team, switching off every minute or two so he can finger her and I can rub her swollen nub. His other hand moves to her breasts. He twirls her nipples and squeezes her tits as her breathing shortens into gasps. I snake my left hand behind her, remembering the way she groaned when Dominic played with her ass. I move a finger underneath to her slick cleft and drag some of her fluid to the back, massaging her puckered flesh. She sticks her ass out, inviting me in.

"You want this?" I ask and she levels her lidded gaze with mine.

"Yes, please," she gasps.

I thrust my index finger into her ass and she welcomes it, pushing back into my hand. It's my turn to finger her, so I alternately pump her ass with one finger and her pussy with two while Caspian rubs her clit.

"Oh, Goddess," she wails, jacking the both of us harder, using my pre-come to intensify the movements.

The three of us climax, all of us moaning, and soon Dom and Thorn join in. All five of us come together in a tsunami of complete and utter ecstasy.

Iphigenia

*I*t was Thorn's idea to cover the entire living room area of his tiny home in futons, mats, blankets, soft material and pillows.

The five of us lay in a cuddle pile together most mornings. I get to choose who I want to sleep in my own bed, in my own tiny home each night. Sometimes I choose one of my men, other times I choose two, three or all four.

In the mornings one guy always makes everyone breakfast and coffee. We like to feed Nolan too. And after that, more often than not, depending on schedules, we traipse together to Thorn's for our group cuddle and talk. We go around in a circle and voice our concerns, if we have any, and work them out. Or we kiss and nap and sometimes a few of us even make love.

With my head in the crook of Thorn's arm, he holds up a hand and juts out his thumb. "Monday I'm taking Iphi sailing on Eli and Ty's boat if anyone else wants to join us."

Rhys snuggles up to my back, spooning me. "I'd like to go."

"Perfect." I crane my head to kiss his soft, warm lips.

Thorn taps his index finger. "Tuesday we're going skydiving. Any takers?"

"I don't have to work on Tuesday so count me in. I'd love to photograph Iphigenia while she does it." Caspian, who's rubbing my feet, pauses to kiss the soles.

I giggle and try to pull a foot away but he holds on to it and goes back to the massage.

"Thursday," Thorn holds up his ring finger, "we're all going to Vegas to get married."

"What?" I shoot straight up.

The men laugh and pull me back down. "Joke, sweetheart." Thorn turns to me, smiling broadly.

Disappointment washes over me.

"Not that we wouldn't all jump at the chance," Dominic says and the others murmur agreement.

"But polyandry is not legal in California," says Caspian.

"Yet," adds Rhys.

I burrow deeper into my men, all of their hands or bodies touching mine. "If it were, my mother would give us her blessing." And who ever saw that coming?

"It certainly seems that way." Dominic presses kisses along my forehead.

I can scarcely believe this is my life. Four perfect men who treat me like the center of their universe. Men who do everything for me and yet let me be my own independent person. Men who accept every aspect of who I am and treat me with the utmost respect. Men who surround me, flatter me, hold me up physically and emotionally. Men who feed my soul and love me unconditionally.

EPILOGUE

Six Months Later
Iphigenia

*I*t's eleven at night when the men and I pile into the circus tent on the pier for a brand-new performance. I came up with the idea a week after my return and pitched it to Serlon, who loved it. A way to keep the circus open all year round and keep most of the crew gainfully employed. I call it Circus After Dark—and I was able to bring on my sisters, Burgundy and her girlfriend, Tiyah.

It's for the over-twenty-one crowd only. Serlon got a liquor license and we offer pairings with each act. I do a very sexy aerial performance, mixing up different apparatuses. I've kept the tricks to a minimum and the visual appeal high. It's more about the flourishes and costumes, or lack thereof, than about exerting massive feats of strength and skill. I also get to expand my experience to the hoop and straps as well as the silks.

The other four girls perform a seductive burlesque act. We draw crowds throughout San Diego County and even Los Angeles and Mexico.

We've only been performing for a few weeks and already we fill the house. Requests from other countries are pouring in, each offering to pay handsomely for our production.

"How's everyone doing?" Serlon taps his cane and fixes his top hat. He may love this more than I do.

"Ready whenever you are," Alexis purrs. She wears a sexy-as-hell red leather corset, black fishnets and six-inch come-fuck-me heels. The woman was born for this and takes her position at center stage, holding her arms out wide.

The thick black curtain rises and the crowd stamps their feet, screaming her name. "Alexis, Alexis, Alexis . . ."

She cocks her head, her black hair falling over one eye, and gives them her Cheshire-Cat-on-steroids grin. "Ladies and gentlemen, are you settled into your seats?"

The crowd shouts their assent.

"Are you ready for some sexy, after dark, fun?"

Cheers and whistles erupt.

The music starts, slow and sultry, and Alexis prances around the stage, posing and pouting. Serlon comes out to more cheers and the two of them engage in a short performance. She reaches for his top hat, and he rolls it down one arm and grabs her hand while the hat rolls onto her arm. She bounces it atop her head. They exchange his cane the same way, twirling and tossing and posing between them. After a few minutes they end with Alexis dipped in his arms. From her position she introduces the burlesque act.

The four girls shuffle onto the stage with their black wooden chairs and proceed to wow the audience in an alluring, sultry dance. Then it's my turn and my hoop drops from the ceiling with me already nested inside, basically wearing lingerie. I shoot out a leg and begin the spin. And even though the audience is a blur as I pose with my arms and legs out, balancing on the metal rim, I can still make out all four of my men perched on the edges of their seats in the front row, wearing ear-to-ear grins.

The entire show lasts ninety minutes and we cycle back and forth between acts, each of us performing three times. By the end, the audience is standing and screaming for more but we stop, knowing they'll keep coming back.

My guys are waiting for me outside on the pier when I exit after changing.

"I don't know how you do it." Dominic leans in and kisses my cheek.

"Do what?" I blink up at him.

"Manage to look even more gorgeous than you did this morning." Thorn takes one of my hands, kissing it.

"Glow as though lit by an inner fire." Caspian takes my other.

"Steal the show." Rhys throws his arms around my waist from behind and squeezes. I shriek in giggles.

"Lucky girl." Burgundy joins us with her lovers, Tiyah and Elijah.

"When are we taking the show on the road?" Sadie and Ryder walk up with Chrys and Carter.

"As soon as Serlon locks down the other venues." I smile at each of them.

"Well you've got four willing roadies to follow you girls to the ends of the earth." Thorn picks me up, twirling me around in a circle before passing me to each of my men for more spins and kisses.

Want a FREE Novella? Fire and Fangs is a sexy, enemies to lovers, multiple partner paranormal with sword-crossing.

Looking for more electrifying reads that will leave you spellbound? Look no further than one (or all) of Chloe Adler's five sizzling paranormal romance series, totaling seventeen delectable books!

Another slow burn multiple partner saga promising a hint of darkness:

Chronicles of Tara starting with Synergist, a fantasy reverse harem with fae. Tara follows Amaya, an unlikely heroine and her five enigmatic heroes.

Fast Burn Darker Multiple Partner Books:
Destiny Chronicles beginning with Descent stars Sydney, a defiant sex worker and her five provoca-tive heroes.

Danger after Dark beginning with Paris (but these can easily be read out of order). Each novella follows a different heroine traveling through Europe and their three dangerous heroes.

Fast Burn Paranormal Romances:
Shadow Sisters begins with Overtaken. Each of these novels follows a different heroine but they are all tied together in a delicious love knot of desire and devotion.

Newsletter: If you're not subscribed to Chloe's newsletter yet, please do join The Edge and receive updates on new releases, Chloe's life in Europe, exclusive author musings, advanced book excerpts and cover reveals.

Follow Chloe on your favorite social media platform or drop her a line, she would love to hear from you!

- Instagram
- TikTok
- Facebook
- Bookbub
- Amazon

- Goodreads
- Email

Your kind words and reviews have lifted my spirits and reminded me why I embarked on this writing journey in the first place.

~ Chloe

ALSO BY CHLOE ADLER

Want more Iphi? You can find her, her family and her friends in the 4 book series Shadow Sisters starting with Mortal Desire!

Want a FREE Novella? Subscribe to Chloe's newsletter!

Fire and Fangs is a sexy, enemies to lovers, multiple partner paranormal with sword-crossing. Subscribe to my newsletter to grab it! https://BookHip.com/QFGLCWZ

Looking for more electrifying reads that will leave you spellbound? Look no further than one (or all) of Chloe Adler's sizzling paranormal romance series, totaling seventeen delectable books!

Fast Burn Paranormal Romances:

All your favorite side characters from Tales from the Edge get their happily ever afters in *Shadow Sisters* beginning with Mortal Desire. Sadie Holt + Ryder. Chrysothemis

Holt + Carter. Jared + Alec. And Burgundy + (you'll have to read it to find out)…

A slow burn multiple partner saga promising a hint of darkness:

Chronicles of Tara starting with Synergist, a fantasy reverse harem with fae. Tara tells the story of Amaya, an unlikely heroine and her five enigmatic heroes.

Fast Burn Darker Multiple Partner Books:

Destiny Chronicles beginning with Descent stars Sydney, a defiant sex worker and her five provocative heroes.

Danger after Dark beginning with Paris (but these can easily be read out of order). Each novella follows a different heroine traveling through Europe and their three dangerous heroes.

Follow Chloe on your favorite social media platform or drop her a line, she would love to hear from you!

- Instagram - @chloeadlerauthor

- TikTok - @chloeadlerauthor
- Facebook - facebook.com/groups/523600161317601
- Bookbub - bookbub.com/profile/chloe-adler
- Amazon - www.amazon.com/stores/Chloe-Adler/author/B06ZZ838HR
- Goodreads - goodreads.com/author/show/16722267.Chloe_Adler
- Pinterest: pinterest.com/ChloeAdlerAuthor/

My sincerest thanks for giving my world a place in your imagination. I look forward to seeing you in our next adventure.

~ Chloe